I0747959

Stone Heart

The Gargoyles of Arrington

Jenn Burke

Copyright © 2023 by Jennifer R.L. Burke. Published by Jenn Burke. All rights reserved. No part of this manuscript may be copied electronically, on paper, or in audio without permission from the author.

Cover art © 2022 Mayhem Cover Creations
https://mayhemcovercreations.com/

Editing by Abbie Nicole

This book is a work of fiction and all names, characters, places and incidents are fictional. Any resemblance to actual people, places, or events is coincidental.

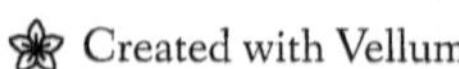 Created with Vellum

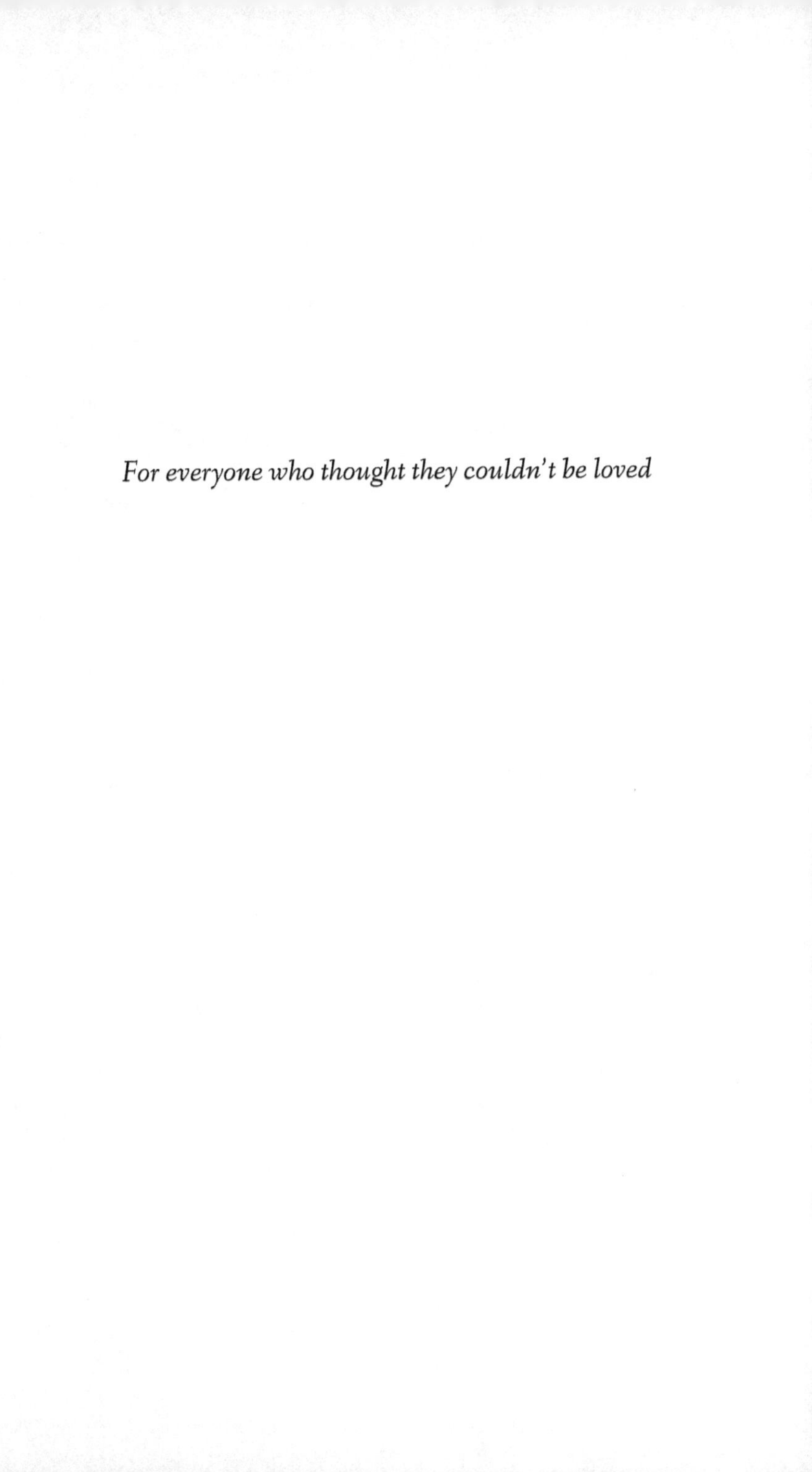

For everyone who thought they couldn't be loved

Chapter 1

Teague

I couldn't keep the sneer off my face as Christian Holt's pet witch made sure their preparations for the unbonding ceremony were properly in place. Normally, I wasn't quite so cynical, but my family—*I*—had already been fooled once by these people. I would probably pay for trusting them again, but what choice did I have?

My brother, Rian, bumped his shoulder against mine. "Stop scowling," he murmured. "Your face will freeze like that."

It was an old joke from our childhood centuries ago, and for a second, my lips threatened to curve upward out of the unpleasant line they'd settled into. I considered bumping him back, but Rian was fully human now, and I was in my living stone form—heavier, denser, stronger than his frail human skin. What I thought to be a gentle bump might send him flying, and I was all too aware of how vulnerable my brothers were now that they'd broken our curse by finding their true loves.

Something that wouldn't happen for me unless this

damned ritual could undo what Christian and his witch had wrought months ago without our knowledge.

Drew, my other brother, leaned around me to glare at Rian. "Let him scowl if he wants. He's entitled to it."

"Thank you," I rumbled, noting Drew's scowl rivaled my own. He'd never fully approved of the plan to bring what we thought were ally werewolves to our territory to prepare for our upcoming hundred-year sleep in stone, particularly because they were descendants of the same pack who'd betrayed us in the eighteenth century. Or supposedly the descendants. As it turned out, they weren't werewolves at all but a sleuth of cursed bear shifters following a prophecy they thought would allow them to break the spell that warped their shifted form into something approximating wolves.

And thus, we were led to this moment of unbonding my soul from Christian Holt's, the lead liar.

He stood across the rough circle, his expression somber as he regarded me. Although I could have singled out his emotions from the mess of everyone else's—anticipation, anger, annoyance, worry—I didn't bother. As always, his appearance was rugged, less than tidy. The bite of the late January air brought up pink spots on the apples of his white cheeks. His brown beard was short but crept downward to join the tuft of hair escaping from the V-neck of his deep-purple Henley. The hair on top of his head was no neater, looking like he'd tumbled out of bed only moments before—but from watching him for months, I knew he didn't style it that way. He wore a black-and-navy-checked flannel and worn jeans, both challenged by the breadth of his biceps and thighs. He was bigger than me in every way, and for a heartbeat of time, I'd thought...

Well, it didn't matter what I'd thought. Not anymore.

Unbidden, my gaze drifted farther around the circle until it fell on Francisco—Frankie. I rather preferred the long version of his name, but he didn't, so I abided by his wishes. He wore a knitted cream toque over his long auburn hair, more for fashion, I suspected, than protection against the chill. As a mountain lion shifter, the cold didn't affect him much. The white skin of his nose and cheeks was flushed pink, and his eyes sparkled as he shared a few words with Chase, the teenager who had escaped the pride with Frankie and three others. Frankie's outfit consisted of a pair of tight black jeans and a cable-knit sweater that matched the color of his toque, and he was so *pretty*. I could look at him all day.

Keelan, the witch, continued with their preparations, and I did my best not to show my impatience. Finally, they seemed satisfied and clapped their hands quietly. "All right, we can—"

Suddenly, the mountain lions' heads jerked up, focused on the driveway. "Expecting anyone?" Frankie asked.

I shared a look with my brothers. "No."

Drew shifted his glare to Chris. "Some latecomers from the ranch?"

"No. Everyone who was planning on being here is here." The other members of his family looked just as puzzled as the rest of us.

Taking a breath, I willed myself into my human skin. The long-sleeved T-shirt I wore suddenly wasn't enough against the cold, but even I could hear the cars now—and yes, there were two—coming up the gravel drive. Confusion and anxiety swirled around me from everyone gathered, but I pushed it aside and headed for the front of the house to greet our visitors.

Partway there, something warm and soft draped itself

over my shoulders. I glanced behind me to see Chris without his flannel. "You'll be cold," I protested.

"Not as cold as you. Your lips are blue."

I frowned at the hyperbole. "They're not. I'm fine."

"Wear it."

"I don't need—"

"Gods' sakes, Teague, wear it before *I* freeze to death looking at you." His glare matched mine.

I would have fought harder, but the vehicles had pulled to a stop and I *was* cold, so I shrugged the shirt on. It was warm from his body heat and smelled of him too—something wild and flowery, which was a surprise—and it made me feel like a kid wearing his father's gambeson for playtime. It was so large on me. Perhaps not the greatest impression for whoever our unexpected visitors were, but...I mentally shrugged. I was thankful I didn't make it a habit to wear my tail out, so there was no awkward tucking that needed to be done before I was presentable to other humans.

My steps faltered as our guests came into view—two Arrington Police Department cruisers. That didn't make sense. If I was needed at work, they would have called, not sent two officers out to notify me. That was a waste of resources.

Both officers exited their vehicles, and I recognized them if not their serious expressions. Olivia Hext loved puns and always had a smile on her face, except now. The other officer, Max Davis, came across to his colleagues as quiet and gentle, though I'd seen him with perps, and he wore a look then much like he wore now.

What was going on?

My anxiety only increased when Olivia's hand hovered over her holstered weapon. "Teague O'Reilly, put your hands in the air where we can see them. Everyone else, move aside."

I complied slowly, my brain too stunned to truly comprehend what was happening. "Olivia, what—"

"Step aside," Max boomed at my brothers, Chris, Frankie, and everyone else. "Move!"

Predictably, Drew didn't listen to the order and stepped in front of me instead. "What is going on?"

"Sir, unless you want to be arrested too—"

"Wait—you're arresting Teague?" That was Frankie's voice from behind me. I didn't look over my shoulder at him. I couldn't. "Why? He's done nothing wrong!"

Max wasn't paying attention to Frankie. His eyes were focused on Drew. "Sir, move aside."

"No."

"Drew, this isn't going to help." I wanted to rest a hand on his shoulder, give him a squeeze, but moving my hands right now also wouldn't help the situation. "Stand down."

He cast a look over his shoulder. "Teague..."

"Whatever this is, we'll figure it out. It's all right."

He looked at me for a second more, his bright-blue eyes boring into mine, before moving aside. Max swept in behind me, grabbed my hands, and held them to the top of my head as he patted me down with his other hand. Once that was done, he pulled my hands to the small of my back and snapped cuffs around my wrists.

"Can I ask why I'm under arrest?" My voice was low, steady, even though I was quaking inside. I didn't understand any of this.

"I'm arresting you for assault. You need not say anything. You have nothing to hope from any promise or favor and nothing to fear from any threat, whether or not you say anything. Anything you say may be used as evidence. It is my duty to inform you that you have the right to retain and instruct counsel in private, without delay. You may call any lawyer you want. If you wish to contact a legal-aid duty lawyer, I can provide you with the telephone number. Do you understand? Do you want to call a lawyer?"

"Yes, he wants to call a fuckin' lawyer," Rian shouted from behind us. "Josh, do you know of someone?"

"On it," came Josh's calm, in-control-of-things voice.

"I got it." Gage, one of Chris's enforcers, stepped up. He looked much like Chris in his T-shirt, flannel, and jeans—a man used to the outdoors.

"You know a lawyer?" Josh asked.

"He *is* a lawyer," Chris corrected. "He practiced when we were in New Brunswick and took the bar in BC last month."

I would never have suspected the hotheaded enforcer was anything but a physical protector, but right now, I wasn't about to look a gift wolf-bear in the mouth. I nodded in acknowledgment. "Thanks. I also want to know the details of the charges against me because I've assaulted no one."

Max nudged me in the direction of his cruiser. "We'll discuss it at the station. Let's go."

"Don't say anything," Gage called after me. "We'll be there soon, and we'll make sense of this."

I appreciated the strength behind his words, but I feared nothing would ever make sense again.

Chapter 2

Chris

It took some fast-talking to convince Teague's brothers to wait at the mansion. Showing up with Teague's entire family wouldn't help matters—if anything, it might piss off his colleagues if we crowded their station. Not to mention Rian and Drew weren't the most emotionally stable regarding their brother. Though I couldn't blame them for that. I got the same way when my sleuth—my family—was threatened.

In the end, it was me, Gage, Logan—Rian's logical professor partner to represent the O'Reillys—and Frankie who headed to the station. We took two vehicles so Gage and I could stop off quickly at the ranch for him to change into a suit, a necessity if we wanted the cops to believe he was truly a lawyer. And he was—I might have lied about a lot of things, but I was done with untruths. They hadn't gotten me anywhere but in a shitload of trouble.

We arrived in the station's parking lot to find Logan's SUV already there. I pulled in beside it as the doors on either side popped open. Logan, a true werewolf who embodied the term *bear* in his human form, was a good choice to be there with us. He was logical and thought with his head rather than his heart, but he cared deeply for his partner's siblings.

Frankie, though...

I swallowed as I caught sight of the petite man, his waist-length auburn hair strikingly red against the cream of his toque and sweater. He grabbed his hair and twisted it over one shoulder, the movement automatic and without thought. I'd noticed he liked to play with it when he was nervous or bored, but boredom usually came with more attention to what he was doing. These movements were all nervousness embodied.

I wanted to pull him into my arms and breathe in his unique scent, but this wasn't the time or place.

"Ready?" Gage asked us, looking the part of the big-city lawyer in his tailored navy suit.

I cast a glance at Logan and Frankie, then nodded. "Ready."

The inside of the police station looked like any you'd see on TV, maybe with a bit less busyness. After all, this was Arrington, a town in the interior of British Columbia, and not New York City. A young man in uniform who looked barely out of his teens sat at the front desk, scowling at something on his computer screen as he chicken-pecked the keyboard. In the background, a phone rang and three people were having a quiet conversation out of sight. The aroma of burnt coffee lingered, along with the sugary yeast of doughnuts. Stereotypes were stereotypes for a reason, I guessed.

Gage waved us to the bench near the front doors and approached the desk. After a handful of seconds where the cop ignored him in favor of whatever he was still trying to type—and I used that term generously—Gage rapped his knuckles on the raised lip of the desk.

"Gage Holt to see Teague O'Reilly. I'm his lawyer."

The cop looked up, his scowl etching deeper into his features. I wasn't sure if it was a reaction to Gage's profession or the mention of Teague, but I wouldn't be surprised if it were the latter. No doubt everyone on the force, small as it was, knew Teague had been charged with assault, though how they could believe it was beyond me.

My fingers clenched into fists where my hands rested against my thighs. I'd known Teague for years, first through correspondence, then these past few months in person. He was always so tightly controlled—there was no way he would assault someone randomly. To protect his family or those he cared about? Yeah. In the line of duty? Hell yeah. But in a way that would see him charged?

It wasn't possible.

A soft touch on my knuckles startled me. I'd been so focused on Gage that I hadn't realized Frankie had chosen the seat next to me. Instantly my fingers uncurled, and I wanted so badly to intertwine his with mine...but we'd agreed. Not until Teague was on board.

"It'll be okay," Frankie murmured, his voice so low I doubted even Logan could hear it on the other side of me.

I swallowed and nodded. It had to be. I had so much to make up for.

Finally, Gage was escorted deeper into the station, and the true torturous waiting began. Logan and Frankie pulled out their phones—Logan to read something that looked way too intense to read on such a tiny screen, and Frankie to watch random short videos. He nudged my shoulder whenever one popped up that was particularly funny, but otherwise, he left me to my thoughts. I had a phone I could pull out too, but I wasn't much of a reader. I didn't want to peruse social media I didn't care about, and I didn't see the point in watching video after video of nonsense. It wasn't for me. I supposed I could play a game of mah-jongg, but that was a game for a few relaxing moments, and this definitely wasn't the time.

After a few more minutes, I pushed to my feet. "Washroom?" I barked at the cop at the front desk. I didn't feel any urgent need to visit it, but it was something to do rather than sit here waiting.

He jerked his head toward a small alcove farther down the hall, his scowl still firmly in place. I didn't bother to thank him since the asshole had clearly already convicted Teague and headed in the direction he'd indicated. The washroom door muffled the station noise, and I appreciated the short reprieve from the unexpected left turn reality had taken.

I was washing my hands when the door opened, unsurprised to see Frankie enter. I watched in the mirror as he approached and plastered himself to my back, his arms wrapped around my middle.

"It'll be okay." He'd said it before, and he said it now with just as much conviction in his voice, muffled as it was against my back. I often forgot Frankie had a petite stature—his personality was always bigger than life—but his head only reached my shoulders.

I shook the water from my hands and dashed them against my jeans to finish drying them enough that I could turn in Frankie's embrace and cup his cheeks with my palms. My fingers trembled as nerves and worry and want collided inside of me in a jumble I couldn't separate. "It has to be," I agreed.

Frankie looked up at me, his glossy pink lower lip caught by too-sharp teeth. "But what if—"

I shook my head. "There's no 'what if.' You and I both know Teague didn't do anything wrong. He couldn't have. He doesn't have it in him to hurt someone without reason."

"I know." Frankie sighed and leaned harder into me. "But I have this niggling feeling that we're missing something."

"The pride's gone. Unless you think one of the survivors decided to bring charges against Teague?"

"No. They were smart enough to walk away from the pride. I can't see them doing something so stupid now." He paused. "Well, maybe. But they wouldn't work through the legal system. They're outlaws, right? They don't trust the cops."

"Fair." I tugged off his toque and swept a long, auburn strand of hair behind his ear. I was dying to comb my hands through his smooth, amazing tresses, but that would have to wait. For the moment, I comforted myself with his scent— crisp, minty, fresh, with a hint of spice...like a mojito on a hot summer's day.

"I think it might be Muirloch."

That name broke through all thoughts about how good Frankie smelled. The idea of the ancient Fomori chased away any good feelings that came from holding him in my arms. "You think?"

His cute nose wrinkled. "She can't work against Teague directly, right? And she doesn't have the pride anymore. So..."

"Shit." He was right—it was a possibility. "Fuck. Why can't she leave them alone?"

Muirloch had been the one to curse them five hundred years ago. She'd helped the brothers' parents, with Teague's hand in marriage as the cost, but the O'Reillys had reneged on the deal. So she'd killed them. She'd been sentenced to death when she was caught, but before the brothers could carry out the sentence, she'd cursed them to be gargoyles. The intervention of their aunt, a powerful witch, had modified the spell somewhat, allowing them to awaken every hundred years for twenty-five, in the hopes they would find their true loves to break the curse. It was only in the past few months that Muirloch had found the brothers and set about taking what she'd been promised—Teague. But she bore her own magical burden and couldn't act directly against anyone, so she was stuck using tools like Frankie's former pride and now, maybe, Arrington PD.

"Because she's a narcissistic cow?" Fire lit Frankie's eyes from within, turning them the orange of his cat for a second. "She wants him, but she can't have him, Chris. I won't let her."

"You and me both, baby." I pulled Frankie closer—only to have him suddenly push out of my arms.

The door opened a second later, and Logan stuck his head in. "Gage wants to talk to us." His eyes lit on Frankie's toque, still in my hand, and I thrust it back at Frankie.

"He was fixing his hair," I explained.

Logan's brow twitched, but he said nothing, merely exited back into the hall.

Frankie grabbed his toque from me, his smile wide and predatory. "You're a shitty liar, Holt."

I sighed. "I know."

Really, the only reason Teague had ever believed me was because he *wanted* to believe me. I'd taken advantage of that, and I hated myself daily for it, especially knowing there was little I could or would change about the past. I needed Teague and his brothers to save my family.

How, I wasn't sure.

WE TOOK the conversation into the parking lot since the weather was still mild and none of us was much affected by the slight chill. Gage loosened his tie and considered leaning against my truck but eyed the winter crud caked on the side and thought better of it. Gotta protect the suit.

"First off, he's fine. He's not freaking out, but he's worried, of course. And confused. I got the sense from the detective handling the investigation that he was also confused, given Teague's exemplary service record."

"Doesn't that count for anything?" I demanded. "How can they believe—"

"They've got video."

The phrase dropped like a bombshell between us, and I sputtered in disbelief. "How?"

"I don't fuckin' know." Gage's lawyer persona fell away, leaving the cousin I'd grown up with—a bit hotheaded, passionate about those he cared for, and not afraid to show his emotions. "They let us see it. It's good quality. Teague's recognizable, in his uniform, and he—" He bit off his words and swept a hand through his short blond hair. "It's a clear assault. Unprovoked. He pushed her against a wall and backhanded her."

"No!" The denial burst out of me, and I spun on my heel to pace away a few steps so I wouldn't take out my rage on the messenger. "There's no way. No. Way."

"Their video says otherwise."

Frankie grabbed my arm and tugged me away from Gage. I hadn't realized I'd gotten so close to him. "Who's the complainant?"

"Moira Lochlan. Ever heard of her?"

Frankie closed his eyes. "Fuck. I was right."

"What?" I asked.

"Moira Lochlan," Logan echoed. "Muirloch."

"What's she look like?" Gage frowned, and I realized he'd never actually seen the Fomori. I'd only caught a glimpse of her during the fight with the mountain lion pride, but it was enough to drill her appearance into my brain.

"Petite, curvy, curly black hair."

He nodded. "Yeah, that was her."

"The footage has gotta be faked somehow," I said. "Not only would he not have attacked her like that, he wouldn't have met her alone." I caught Logan's eye. "Would he?"

He started to shake his head, then hesitated. "I'd like to think not, but the man makes...interesting decisions sometimes."

He was stubborn as hell too, and if he thought he was protecting his family... "What a mess."

"Next steps?" Frankie still held on to my arm. I didn't think anyone else noticed, and I certainly wasn't going to encourage him to let go.

"They're going to release him today with a promise to appear. I'm not sure when the preliminary hearing will be—it depends on the court's case load. A couple of weeks, maybe."

Frankie let out a relieved breath. "So he's coming home today."

"Yes. He'll be on administrative leave with pay, and he'll have some restrictions about being in contact with the complainant—"

"Like they've ever sought her out." I snorted.

Gage raised a brow in acknowledgment. "Your job will

be keeping Teague and the brothers from going after Muirloch. Now that the legal system is involved, we *can't* do any vigilante shit."

I gritted my teeth. "That's bullshit."

He lifted his hands, palms out. "She's the one who changed the game. Now we have to play along. If she doesn't appear for the court proceedings, and there's any hint Teague might have had something to do with that—it will ruin his last two years as a cop."

"No, it'll ruin *him*," Frankie corrected softly.

Yeah, it would. Honor and integrity meant everything to Teague. That didn't mean he was a saint—he'd sin as fast as any of us if it meant protecting his family—but he had a code he lived by. Damaging that publicly would mess with his sense of self.

"You all head back. I'll escort him home. It'll probably be an hour or so while they get the paperwork ready." Gage held up his hand, and I tossed the truck keys to him without hesitation.

"Let me know if anything changes," I said.

"I will," he promised. Striding forward, he wrapped one arm around me and pulled me close. A brief, hard gesture of family that we rarely shared—not because we didn't love each other, but because our family had never been huge on physical shows of affection, thanks to the example set by my asshole father. "We're gonna make sure he gets through this," Gage whispered.

I nodded and patted his back with the arm Frankie wasn't holding. I couldn't say anything. I tried, but my voice wouldn't come.

All I could think was that Gage held my future—and maybe his own—in his hands.

Chapter 3

Frankie

I will cut a bitch.

The mantra ran through my head as I kneaded the bread dough. Nikki had taken one look at our faces when Logan, Chris, and I walked in and set us all to work. Logan, she sent off to the guesthouse, where Rian was already tasked with cleaning out the second bedroom that had been used as a storage space but had a future as Logan's home office so he could continue with his job at UVic once his year-long sabbatical was done. Chris, she shooed outside to chop firewood—something I wouldn't have minded watching, honestly, especially if he got overheated and had to strip off his shirt...

Ahem.

With the other two occupied, she set a recipe book in front of me on the kitchen counter and instructed me to make bread.

Maybe not the best choice considering how murderous I was feeling.

Usually, I found baking instructions soothing. There was an order to it, a logical science, that appealed to me. I could follow the steps and control the outcome. Nikki knew this, which was probably why she'd given me this task and not something potentially destructive like, say, chopping firewood. I could do that as easily as I could bake bread, but letting me loose with a sharp implement right now was not a good plan.

I was over-kneading the dough, but you know what? I didn't fucking care. How *dare* she? Muirloch. Bitch extraordinaire. None of us had ever considered she'd get the human authorities involved in the made-up dispute she had with the brothers, but I supposed we should have thought she'd do something. She couldn't take direct action against the brothers, thanks to her own curse of impotence. No killing them herself, which was why she'd manipulated my old pride into doing her dirty work. Now the pride was gone, and she was left with nothing. Except for a police force willing to believe the worst of one of its own.

I slapped the dough against the counter, accidentally catching the edge of a metal mixing bowl with my hand. It clanged sideways, rolling along the stone before clattering to the floor and scattering the bit of flour left in it across a few square feet of tile. Nikki scooped the bowl off the floor, set it carefully back on the counter, then eyed me like a mother would.

Mothers on TV and in books, anyway. I couldn't remember my own mother giving me that judgy-but-caring look.

Nikki absently brushed the flour off the brown skin of her hands onto her apron. "Get it out of your system?"

I punched the dough. "No."

"Good thing I'm not actually depending on that bread for dinner." She smirked. "Abuse it to your heart's content."

I picked it up and slapped it on the counter again, then

sighed. Maybe I had gotten it out of my system after all. "I just feel so...so..."

"Helpless?" Her smirk faded, replaced by a look that told me she knew exactly how I felt.

Of course she did.

Nikki, Sarah, Henry, Chase, and I had been the lowest of the low in the pride. Becker had adhered to a stupid hierarchical structure of value, assigning worth to someone based on their role in the group. Nikki and Sarah had looked after the food and were female—*misogynistic gasp*—so, therefore, they were lesser. Chase was young and eager to be ordered around, but also an awkward, gangly teen without the coordination to ride a motorcycle, despite being a shifter, so he didn't even have the protection of the title of future biker. Henry was the pride's mechanic and should have been respected—he looked after their rides, after all—but because of his age, he was ridiculed instead. Never let it be said the pride had understood the saying *don't shit where you eat.*

And me? I did whatever Becker told me to do. Because in the pride, I was always as helpless as I felt right now. I never had control over any part of my life then.

I fucking *hated* it.

The sound of Chris's truck coming up the drive completely distracted me from the abused dough. I looked at the mess on my hands and the mess on the counter, and Nikki took pity on me.

"Go get cleaned up. I'll take care of this and get Chase to round everyone up."

I kissed her on the cheek. "Thanks, Nik."

Wiping the worst of the drying dough from my hands onto the apron, I tossed it in the laundry room and raced up the stairs to change into clothes that didn't have flour on them. The apron had protected me from getting totally flour-covered, but stray bits had still ended up on my pants and T-shirt. Once in the room I shared with Chase, I stripped, stowed my discarded clothes in the hamper, and forced myself not to think too hard about what I should wear. I washed up, then chose a different pair of jeans and a T-shirt, this one a deep emerald that brought out the green in my eyes. Simple. I did take the time to twist a knot into the front of the overlarge T-shirt so it didn't hang shapelessly on my slim body, but that was about all the fashion I had time for. I freed my hair from its messy topknot and brushed it out, and that was it. I was ready.

At least in appearance.

Was I ever truly ready to see Teague?

From the moment I'd first met him, the night we'd escaped the pride, my cat had recognized him as someone special. I hadn't understood what that meant at the time. Us mountain lions, we didn't have the whole "mates" thing werewolves did—or, at least, that's what I'd always believed. There certainly wasn't any mystique around finding a partner in the pride or outside of it. But my cat had growled *this one* at me, and it had taken time for me to realize what he meant.

Then Chris had come to the brothers' New Year's Eve party—mostly because Josh had insisted he be invited—and my cat had growled *this one* again. Which, honestly, was confusing as fuck but also as selfish as I had come to expect my beast to be. Of course it wanted two guys now that I was free from the confines of the pride and Becker's control.

But that *this one* had been reciprocated by Chris's wolf-bear, and he'd explained what it meant.

Mates.

Chris was my mate. Teague was too. It was the same for

Chris. Now we just had to convince Teague that he didn't actually hate Chris—debatable—and that I wasn't too young for him—because I knew that was what he thought every time he looked at me. The whole unbinding thing was supposed to have been the first step in giving Teague the freedom to start coming around to liking Chris again. We thought we'd have two years to convince him Chris wasn't a bad guy—but with Muirloch's interference, we might only have two weeks. Because if Teague got convicted…

Shit, no. I wasn't going to think that.

I flipped my hair over my shoulders and trotted downstairs in time to see Teague's brothers greeting him at the front door. He looked…haggard. He still wore Chris's giant flannel shirt, and it didn't do him any favors. His human skin didn't hide the stress lines etched around his mouth nor the dark circles under his eyes. He returned his brothers' hugs, but it was a by-rote gesture. His purple-tinged blue eyes were distant, as though he were still sitting in a cell in his own police station.

What a fucking insult that had to have been.

I hopped down the last few steps on my way in for my own greeting. Opening my arms, I pulled him down for a hug. Unlike Chris, Teague was only two or three inches taller than me, which made hugging him much more comfortable for both of us. "I'm glad you're back," I said softly, almost in his ear.

As I'd hoped, he shivered, even as he patted me on the back and pulled away. He wasn't unaffected by me, but what he wanted was buried so far beneath his honor and what he thought he should do that it would take something of a miracle to get him thinking differently. With a forcibly shortened timeline, I didn't know how Chris and I were going to pull it off.

I also wasn't going to think about what would happen if we didn't.

The back patio door opened, and Chris walked in, finishing pulling on his shirt. Dammit, he *had* taken it off. I'd yet to see his broad chest without anything covering it, but I could picture it—broad, muscular, his pecs and stomach covered in a pelt of hair that only enhanced his masculinity. Something I could run my fingers through or feel the roughness of against my own lean, hairless chest. It was enough to make my mouth water.

Chris knew it too, given the heated look he shot me. "Wood's chopped."

Oh, I *bet* I could chop his wood.

Teague scowled at Chris's entry but didn't tell him to get out. Progress? "We all need to talk."

"Chris too?" I tried not to sound too eager at the prospect, but maybe his attitude toward Chris had softened more than I'd thought if he was being invited to family meetings.

"Chris too. We're going to need his family's help."

Oh. Yeah, there was that.

We gathered in the living room. There wasn't enough seating for everyone, but that never bothered us. We all took turns sitting on the floor, and we kept our human forms to do it. That was one rule Josh had implemented straightaway —shifters in animal forms weren't allowed in the living room. Turns out, magical mountain lions and wolves were too big for indoors. Especially all at one time.

Drew directed Teague to one of the armchairs. Teague often chose to sit on the floor, but I was glad to see we all agreed he wouldn't today. He'd had an uncomfortable enough day already.

When we were seated, Teague heaved a breath. "I need to go away."

Gage—who I hadn't realized had stayed rather than going back to the ranch—spoke up immediately. "You have to appear for the initial hearing—"

Teague waved a hand. "I know. I'm not talking about disappearing permanently."

"Thank fucking god," Rian breathed, leaning into Logan, who was sitting on the couch behind him with his legs on either side of Rian as he sat on the floor.

"Sorry. Let me clarify." Teague winced apologetically, no doubt feeling the strong emotional objections of all of us at the thought of him leaving. He closed his eyes for a moment, and when he opened them, there was more than an apology in them—there was regret. "The tape they showed us was tampered with, Gage, to suggest I assaulted Muirloch, but the meeting...that did happen."

"What the fuck, Teague?" Drew exploded upward and paced away a few steps, toward the foyer, before spinning around. "You met with her?"

"And you didn't tell us?" Rian added.

I held myself still, contained, though the thought of Teague being so close to the creature who wanted him to be hers—who thought he rightfully *belonged* to her—made my insides alternately boil and freeze. "What were you thinking?" I whispered.

I sought the comfort of Chris's gaze across the room, but he glared at Teague from where he stood near the dining room wall, his arms crossed and shoulders bunched like he was ready to attack something. He said nothing, but he didn't need to—his expression shouted his opinion about Teague's actions. An opinion I was sure we all shared.

I knew I did. Such a stupid move.

"I definitely wasn't thinking she'd get security footage and find someone who could manipulate it," Teague admitted with a sigh. "Honestly, I thought meeting there was safest because I knew there were cameras at that convenience store, and it would protect me."

"Críost, Tadgh." The Irish rolled off Drew's tongue so easily. I often forgot that English wasn't the brothers' first language—they barely had an accent unless they were emotional or tired, or drunk, as I'd discovered on New Year's Eve.

"Explain how this ties into you 'going away,'" Logan prompted, ever the logical wolfy.

"She gave me an ultimatum when I met her—either I went with her, or she'd make my life miserable. I had assumed she meant she'd come after Drew and Rian. She knows they broke the curse and that they're human." He turned sad eyes on his brothers. "That's why I asked you to be extra careful. I never thought she'd take this action instead. It didn't once cross my mind that she'd risk getting the human authorities involved."

"Still doesn't explain why you need to go away," Drew grumbled.

"To protect you."

"Oh, you scut." Rian jerked forward, but Logan dropped a hand on his shoulder, and he settled back. "That's a shite reason, and you know it."

"Hear me out, all right? I had nothing but time to think about this in that goddamned cell. Drew, for gods' sakes, will you sit down?" He waited until Drew did so, grudgingly, then continued, "There has to be a reason she went after me rather than you two. She knows the quickest way to get me to capitulate would be to threaten you, and let's be honest—you're far more vulnerable now that you're fully human."

"We've got our magic—"

Teague cut Drew off. "I know, but you're still human. All it would take would be for her to hire someone handy with a rifle and set up in the woods around the mansion." Like the pride had done months ago to mess with the brothers and Chris. "Why hasn't she done that? Maybe it comes down to her own curse."

"Impotence." Logan tilted his head back and forth as he considered it. "Could be. You're suggesting that maybe part of her curse is that she can take any sort of action against someone only once?"

"Exactly. She's already acted against Drew and Rian—the curse."

I shook my head. "The same applies to you though. If she can't act against them, she shouldn't be able to act against you."

"No, no…I see where he's coming from," Logan said. "She can't kill directly—that's the curse of her impotence. The curse to turn the brothers into gargoyles was her solution to 'kill' them—she couldn't kill Drew and Rian outright, and she wanted to freeze Teague so she could retrieve him later. Your aunt interfered with that plan by modifying the spell so you'd awaken on your own without Muirloch undoing it."

"Which she would have done for only Teague," I clarified.

Logan nodded.

"Well. Thank the gods for Aunt O'Reilly then."

Rian lifted a fist for me to bump, and I did so.

"My point is, if she's focused on me, there's a chance anyone associated with me might become collateral damage.

I don't want that. So, for the next two weeks, I'm going to go."

"If you say you're going to set yourself up as bait to keep her away from us..." Drew let his menacing growl fade.

"No. I want to disappear off her radar."

"And you don't think she'll turn her frustrations on anyone in this room?" It was the first time Chris spoke, and nothing about his demeanor said he was on board with Teague's plan.

"That's why I was hoping your...uh, Keelan, would do a casting of protection for the household. If they can."

Chris rolled one shoulder, the movement stiff with tension. "I can ask."

"Where are you planning to go?" Josh asked softly.

"Gale Collingwood, my partner—" Teague paused as his brothers and Josh nodded, so I assumed they'd all met her. "When I got my phone back, she'd blown it up with texts. All supportive." By the softness in his purple-tinged eyes, I could tell it meant a lot to him that not every cop he knew assumed he was guilty. "She offered her husband's cousin's off-grid hunting cabin if I wanted to get away. I'm going to take her up on it."

"It's not far then?"

"Northwest of Clearwater. Close enough that if anything happens, I can be home fairly quickly, but far enough that I hope she won't try to find me."

Drew grunted. "Doubt you'll have cell coverage, so you'll need to go into Clearwater to text us regularly."

"I can do that."

Some tension left Drew's shoulders, which told me he was done fighting with his brother on this. Rian looked at Logan, who ran a large hand over the red hair where Rian once sprouted horns—a gargoyle feature long gone now that he was human. After closing his eyes for a second, Rian opened them and sighed.

"I guess you're going on vacation then." He didn't sound happy about the idea, but then, I didn't think any of us were.

Part of being in a pride—or a pack or a sleuth—was safety in numbers. Wild mountain lions were solitary creatures, socializing with others in their community area only rarely, but our human side told us shifters the importance of being in a group. We could only do so much alone. The idea of Teague running off to be on his own, without the protection of his family, didn't sit right with me. In fact, it made all the tiny little hairs on the back of my neck and along my spine stand on edge. If I were in my cat form, it would be obvious from my hackles that I was not happy at all.

I glanced at Chris, and from the way he couldn't quite stand still, he was equally uncomfortable. The movements were subtle, but there—a shifting of his feet, his fingers flexing where they rested on his elbows, his twitching brows. Our eyes met, and I saw the same determination in them that I felt.

Wherever Teague was going, he wasn't going alone.

Chapter 4

Teague

I was exhausted. More than that, I was numb.

It was shock. I'd experienced it enough in my life that I easily recognized it—the feeling that the world around me wasn't quite real, as well as the distance from my emotions and those around me, as though I were blanketed by an invisible fog. Thinking took effort, but if there was anything I was good at, it was functioning when I was in the middle of a crisis.

I'd never had a choice. As the oldest brother, I was the one Drew, Rian, Odhrán, and Finnian had all turned to when our parents were killed. Or when we'd first awoken as monsters. Or when we awoke the next time to find Odhrán was nothing more than dust. I was the one they leaned on, relied on, so I had to keep us moving forward.

But this time, the loss was so much more mine alone.

My career.

When I'd awoken early in 1997, it had been a shock to everyone. Glenn Pallesen, Josh's father, had been our care-taker then, and he'd scrambled to get me all the modern identification I needed two years ahead of schedule. It would have been easy to make a business for myself like Drew and Rian eventually did, but no, I had to be difficult and enter the police academy—after I'd taken the time to acclimate myself to the new century I'd found myself in. But I couldn't *not* do it, now that it was an option. It was the role I was born for. Back in our natural lifetime, I was a protector for our king. Once I learned I could be that for this adopted town of ours, I'd needed to.

And now, nearly twenty years of work, blood, sweat, and a few tears, were all tossed away by a creature bent on owning something she had no right to. Me.

I shoved the last of my clothes into the duffel and zipped it closed. Casting a final glance around my room to make sure I wasn't forgetting anything, I shoved down the thought that I wouldn't see it again. Of course I would. This trip was temporary. I wasn't in love with the idea of going off on my own—I hadn't been truly alone in...well, *ever*—but it remained the only reasonable idea to protect my brothers and this family we'd created for ourselves. If I wasn't here, they couldn't get caught in the crossfire, and I prayed Muirloch would be so consumed with trying to find me that she'd forget about everything else.

If she didn't, that's what Keelan's protective spell was for. They'd already cast it, anointing everyone's foreheads with some fragrant mixture and a few low words I couldn't follow. They'd insisted on doing the same to me, even though I had protested that their magic needed to be reserved for the others. That comment had earned a light smack to the back of my head from Frankie, a scoff from Keelan, and a low growl from Chris, so I'd given in. I hadn't felt much different afterward, still buffered by shock, but a slight sense of rightness calmed my soul somewhat and let me breathe more deeply.

Whether it was the spell or a placebo effect, I didn't know, but I'd take it.

I hefted my duffel onto my shoulder and left my room, closing the door with a final-sounding click. Shrugging off the foreboding, I made my way downstairs, unsurprised to see my family gathered there. Drew with his arm around Josh. Rian leaning against Logan, who towered over all of us. Nikki and Sarah wiping away tears. Chase, a normally incorrigible teenager, was subdued for once and standing close to Henry, the grizzled old mechanic who was happy to belong somewhere good and welcoming.

And then there were Frankie and Chris. Who...had duffel bags of their own?

"No." I halted at the foot of the stairs and glared daggers at the two of them. "You need to stay here, where you're safe, and you can—"

"Shut up, Teague." Frankie flipped his hair over his shoulder. "You're not going alone."

Shock froze my tongue for a second, but that was enough time for Drew to jump in. "You want us to be safe? We want the same for you. So you take Frankie and"—he swallowed and managed to continue through gritted teeth—"*Chris* or you don't go. Simple."

I let my bag drop to the floor with a thud. "That wasn't the agreement."

"What agreement?" Rian asked. "You told us what you were going to do. Now we're telling you."

I clenched my jaw. Taking Frankie wasn't...ideal, but I could handle that. I liked him. A lot. I'd seen how he looked at me occasionally, and while being stuck with him in a cabin for two weeks might give him the wrong idea, I was sure we could have a good discussion and work things out. Chris, on the other hand...

Looking at him still hurt.

"I know." Chris's soft but firm words drew my attention, and he continued, "But I promised I would make amends to your family, and this is how I can start doing that. I'll protect you with my life."

I recoiled at that idea. The thought of him getting hurt for me...no. "You don't need to—"

"I do," he insisted. "Once we get there and get settled, Keelan will come and set up the unbonding again. There are calculations and shit, apparently, depending on the location, the date, and so on. Who knew there was so much math in magic?"

I felt my lips twitch in spite of myself. Who knew, indeed. It pointed to how powerful my aunt had been that she could modify Muirloch's spell without any sort of prep.

"So?" Rian prompted. "You good?"

I looked at my gathered family and the determination on their faces and knew this was a battle I wasn't going to win. It was my turn to be protected, and how could I argue their love for me? It was all there for me to sense, pounding at the foggy blanket separating me from the world—their love, their caring, their concern. I let the warmth of it wrap around me and comfort me as it was meant to. My tail twitched from its usual hiding place, wrapped around my waist, and I knew the damn thing wanted to wag.

"I'm good," I said, then glanced at Frankie and Chris, whose expressions were starting to lighten from the near-scowls they'd been wearing. "*We're* good."

I hoped I wasn't lying.

THE DRIVE to the cabin took a bit longer than the estimated three and a half hours. We were squished into the front seat of Chris's truck—Frankie was in the middle, acting as a buffer between Chris and myself—and the ride was mostly silent, other than the radio playing at a low volume. I was too tired to keep up a conversation, and I didn't know what to say, anyway. We didn't talk much when we stopped in Clearwater to get groceries and other supplies, either, other than to confirm what meals we planned to have over the next week or so.

By the time we found the cabin, down a rutted lane bordered in snow at the base of trees where the sun clearly didn't reach, daylight was nearly gone, the forest and mountains making night come on more quickly than I was used to. There was no sound other than what the truck generated —the low rumble of its engine and the gentle splash of tires through the slushy puddles gathered in the tracks etched into the lane. I wasn't sure about the others, but I was almost holding my breath as we waited for the cabin to come into view, and even though I hadn't been on board with the idea of Chris and Frankie coming with me, I was suddenly glad for their presence.

If I'd arrived in the darkness by myself, I wasn't ashamed to admit I might have turned around and gone back home. I needed to be away from Arrington, but this was *away*. I would have been in true solitude like I'd never experienced.

The truck's headlights swung over the cabin as we rounded a curve in the lane, offering enough illumination to see the building clearly despite the deepening twilight.

"Oh, it's cute," Frankie said, sounding surprised and a little breathless. Maybe he'd been holding his breath.

He wasn't wrong. It was all honey-colored wood, with a

wraparound porch that was probably a great place to sit and have a coffee as the sun came up. The roof hung low over the porch, ensuring that we'd be able to use it, rain or shine, and a chimney made of rough stone jutted from the left side of the small structure. A couple of blue-tinged solar-powered lights stuck out of patches of snow close to the steps that led up to the porch, helping to delineate them from the rest of the dark yard. There were no other lights outside that I could see. The wall facing the front drive had enough space for a door and a picture window, illustrating that this was a *tiny* cabin.

Which...hadn't really occurred to me when I'd agreed to allow Chris and Frankie to accompany me.

"It's small," Chris said, without any of the appreciation that had been in Frankie's words.

Yes. Yes, it was.

Shite.

Frankie patted Chris's arm. "It'll be fine. I mean, if there's only one bed, we can let Teague have it. We'll shift and sleep on the floor."

Chris grunted and put the truck into Park while I was stuck on the thought of *only one bed*. There couldn't be just one bed, right? This was a hunting cabin, and, presumably, the owner didn't come up here alone for his hunting excursions. There would be bunks, surely?

It turned out to be even worse than that.

Since I had the keycode for the battery-powered lock, I entered the cabin first and froze a few steps into the interior. Oh no.

Frankie pushed by me and huffed a breath. "Huh. One room, eh?"

That was it. A double bed was tucked into the left corner farthest from the door, next to the fireplace. A well-worn blue-and-green plaid chair was on the wall opposite the bed, closest to the door, and a matching sofa faced the fireplace. In the back right corner was an area I guessed was the kitchen, with a rough-hewn pine table jutting out from the wall. There was a rope attached to the end, and it took me a second to realize that the table didn't have any legs—it was held in place by the rope hanging from the ceiling. A couple of equally rough stools were tucked underneath the table.

"Uh..." Chris was scowling at the kitchen, which had a distinct lack of a sink. Instead, there was a basin sitting on the counter. "Where's the bathroom?"

"There's an outhouse," Frankie said. "I saw it behind the cabin as we pulled in."

"What?" That was definitely a whine in Chris's voice.

Frankie squinted at him. "What did you think 'off-grid' meant?"

"Solar powered."

"With these trees?" Frankie scoffed. "No way."

"I *hate* outhouses," Chris grumbled.

"You're a bear. Go shit in the woods."

He invited himself up here, knowing how I felt about him, and now he was going to complain about a lack of facilities? His dislike of the situation poked at my senses, making me extra irritable. "You can always turn around and head back to Arrington."

"Like hell." He pushed past Frankie and me, aiming for the "living room." "I'll take the couch."

He set his duffel on it as though either Frankie or I would dare claim it once he'd said something. I rolled my eyes and turned to Frankie. "You want the bed?"

"No, man. I'll take the floor in front of the fireplace. As long as we keep the fire going, my cat will be perfectly content. *Purrrfectly.*" He grinned, inviting me to share the joke, and I couldn't help but return his smile.

I really did like him a lot.

It felt wrong to take the only bed in the cabin, but there was no point in arguing with Frankie, and I wasn't going to try to convince Chris he should be more comfortable. As far as I was concerned, he should be as uncomfortable as possible, twenty-four hours a day, seven days a week, until I decided he'd paid enough penance. I had no idea how long that would be—maybe the one-hundred-and-twenty-seven years he'd pledged his "pack" to protect my family.

Maybe double since it had been a lie.

I sucked in a long, slow breath and let it out just as slowly as I set my duffel on the bed. The best thing to do was ignore him as best I could. Be cordial—there was no point in making things more difficult than they had to be by being outright hostile—but otherwise, pretend he wasn't even there.

Light suddenly flooded the cabin, and I turned to find Frankie triumphantly examining a newly lit oil lamp on the side table next to the couch. That one light was enough to illuminate every corner of the cabin, confirming how small the space was. It would've been ideal for me alone but with the addition of Frankie and Chris? For two weeks?

I hoped all of us came down from the mountain intact.

Chapter 5

Chris

The cabin wasn't any bigger in the light of day.

I woke up first—well, it would be more accurate to say I decided to get up first since I hadn't truly slept all night. Fits and starts of dozing, that was all. The couch was not at all comfortable. I'd follow Frankie's example and shift tonight to sleep more easily on the floor.

Though I hated shifting if I didn't need to. It always felt so wrong, being in a form that was a bastardization of what my beast should be. Still, if I slept better, it might be worth it.

I trekked to the outhouse—*Jesus Christ*, it was cold—then spent a good few minutes trying to convince my penis that it didn't have to hide inside my body so I could actually do what I needed to do. When I returned to the cabin, Frankie was still curled up near the hearth, a giant ball of tawny fluff. His eyes were closed, but his ears twitched, following me as I puttered in the kitchen to make a peanut butter sandwich. Teague was a lump under wool blankets—I could see his dark brown hair and a gray-toned ear and cheek, and that was it.

Unlike me, he'd slept soundly all night. I'd listened to his slow, even breathing, glad he'd found himself able to rest and hoping it would lull me to sleep as well. It hadn't worked, but I was in a new location, deep in the wilderness, and despite being a shifter who was used to rural living, I wasn't used to having only two other people with me.

I missed the sounds of my family. Even in the middle of the night at the ranch, there was always noise—snoring, the gentle murmurs of night owls watching TV, the enthusiastic bed-creaking of couples making love. Here, it might as well have been silent for all the presence Teague and Frankie had while asleep. Instead, the sounds of nature crept in. Owls hooting, bushes rustling, the wind making tree branches knock together.

I didn't like it. Honestly, I didn't really like nature all that much, at least not the untamed version that surrounded us. Give me a nicely populated rural homestead any day over this...nothingness.

With power. And internet. And fucking *running water*.

Movement caught my eye, and I watched Frankie rise to his feet, stretching. He shifted back to human, the transformation much faster and smoother than mine. When his pale human skin came into sight, I knew I should tear my gaze away, but I couldn't. His lithe form was beautiful—his lean muscles toned, not bulky like mine, and I longed to run my hands over his peaches-and-cream skin. His auburn hair reached the top of his buttocks, almost like an arrow pointing to their perfection.

Only when he pulled on his athletic pants did I look away and focus on finishing my sandwich.

When he turned around, pulling a T-shirt over his chest, he smirked and walked over to me. "Enjoy the show?"

he asked, his voice pitched low, as he snatched up the second half of my breakfast and downed it in a couple of bites.

I hummed appreciatively. "You know I did."

His smirk widened into a smile, and he popped up on his toes to kiss my cheek. "Want coffee?"

"Gods, yes."

A few minutes later, we were situated on the porch, a percolator bubbling away on a camp stove I hadn't even realized was there. Frankie had gotten everything going as though he was used to camping—hell, maybe he was. For all the chemistry crackling between us and the time we'd spent getting to know each other at the New Year's Eve party a month ago, I didn't know enough about his history. His story.

But I wanted to.

He curled up in the Muskoka chair next to mine, angling toward me, the blanket he'd grabbed from the couch wrapped around him. The pale winter sun was starting to lighten the forest around us, but a deep chill still permeated the air. It took me only a few seconds to decide I needed my own blanket, so I grabbed the second one I'd been using overnight and wrapped it around myself. Once the coffee was ready and I held the warm mug, it would be a decent morning.

"You look grumpy." Frankie kept his voice low so we wouldn't disturb Teague, but with the door and windows closed, we didn't have to whisper. "Didn't sleep well?"

"New place," I said with a shrug. I didn't want to go into the details of what I'd missed through the night.

"Yeah, I know. It always takes a few days to adjust, especially if you're used to the noise of people."

I grimaced. "Am I that much of an open book?"

He shook his head, smiling softly. "No, just a guess. When I was a kid, there were a few times Mom and I ended up crashing in cabins off-season. After being in a city or town, the mountains would seem so...intense."

"The quiet."

"Exactly. Except then you realize it's not really all that quiet, and that's a whole new level of adjustment."

"You seem to know your way around roughing it." I nodded in the direction of the camp stove.

"Some skills you never forget." His hazel eyes lost some of their sparkle, but he quickly shook himself out of whatever dark space he'd gone to. "I'm going to guess you never went camping as a kid."

"Maybe once or twice? I don't remember much except for roasting wieners and marshmallows over a campfire."

He chuckled. "The important stuff."

"Yeah. I was pretty young—maybe six or so. Before my dad got bored with being a dad and spent more time trying to find people to fuck rather than paying attention to me."

Shit, why had I gone there?

Frankie's smile died away. "I'm sorry."

"No, I am." I sighed. "No one needs to hear me whine about that. He's been gone thirty years. You'd think I would have let that resentment go."

"Eh, I think that sort of resentment sticks with you forever." The percolator made a noise, and Frankie hopped to his feet to take it off the burner before it could disturb our sleeping gargoyle.

As he poured the coffee into two enamel camp mugs, then handed one to me, I considered his words. He'd spoken them with the weight of experience. Once he returned to his seat and rearranged the blanket, I ventured, "Your mom?"

He nodded, his mug cradled in his hands. "She loved me, I know that. But she couldn't make a good decision to save her life." He let out a soft breath and added, "Literally."

I winced. "Sorry."

"It was a long time ago. She got involved with a bad pride, made shitty decisions, and...died. When I was ten. After that, I got passed around from pride to pride."

"Oh, man. That's rough." My dad had been a horrible man, but at least when he'd gotten himself killed, I had family to take me in and protect me.

"It was. But it made me strong. Resilient." His expression reflected the strength he held within, and his eyes flashed orange for a bare second. "I could have let it beat me down, but I chose to let the challenges shore me up instead. I'm proud of who it made me."

"Even if you wonder what might have been, right?"

"Yeah," he admitted. "But that way lies madness."

I lifted my mug out to him, and he tapped the rim of his against it. "Here's to that."

I preferred my coffee with cream, not only the sugar Frankie had added, but we'd forgotten to grab some in Clearwater. I'd live without it, but damn, this camp brew was strong. The aroma was comforting, though, and the hit of caffeine was welcome after my sleepless night. Around us, birds began to chirp, greeting the sun as it rose higher, and it was almost enough to make me think spring was on its way...except for the snow I could scent in the air.

"What's our plan?"

I didn't pretend to not know what he meant. "We've got two weeks. Maybe a little less."

"I wanted to take our time. Ease him into the idea of liking you again."

I scratched my fingernails through my beard. "I'm not sure two years would be enough for that. I fucked up."

"You really did."

Despite the reservations of Keelan and other family members, the ruse had been the only option that made sense to me. After all, despite chatting with Teague for a few years, on and off, I didn't *know* him. All I knew was that this was a family who'd once worked with the despicable MacGrath pack, and what sort of terrible people would affiliate themselves with a werewolf pack who was cruel, dishonest, and manipulative?

As it turned out, a family who was desperate and innocent. But I didn't know that until after I'd put my plans into motion. Keelan had insisted that their prophecy about the three O'Reilly brothers leading us home didn't require any sort of bonding, but I'd been worried about retaliation. So I'd asked them to bond my soul to Teague's, to give us time to figure out what the prophecy meant. Everything would have been fine except for two things. One, Logan Davis, professor and actual werewolf, who'd almost immediately recognized that we weren't true wolves, and two, the spell might have inadvertently blocked Teague from finding his true love and breaking his curse.

Though...he was meant to be with Frankie and me. I felt it deep in my bones, a longing that equaled the pull that tugged me toward Frankie. So did it matter if we kept the bond in place? Would it help him see that Frankie and I were his true loves? If we broke it, would it break the true-love thing?

I didn't know. The problem was Keelan didn't either.

And Teague hated me because of what I'd forced on him—rightfully so.

Yeah, I'd fucked up *royally*.

"We need to win him over," Frankie said. "You've got to stop your growly-scowly act."

"My what?"

He rolled his eyes. "Fuckin' alpha males. You need to open up. Be vulnerable."

"Uh…"

He placed his mug on the table between our chairs. "Gods. Okay. Let's practice."

"Let's what?"

"Pretend I'm Teague."

"Why?"

He threw his head back. "Work with me here. I'm Teague."

"Uh…okay." I frowned. "I'm still me, right?"

"Yes, you're you." His lips twitched like he was holding back a smile. Then he deepened his voice, which I guess was supposed to mimic Teague's? "I'm really pissed at you for bonding our souls."

What was I supposed to do here? "I'm sorry?"

"Ugh. No." Frankie let out an exasperated breath. "You've apologized a million times already. He knows you regret it. Maybe that wasn't the best place to start." He tugged on a strand of his hair as he thought for a moment. "Okay, how about this. We're sitting on the porch."

"Yes, we are. Are you you, or are you Teague?"

"I'm Teague. It's a quiet moment, just the two of you."

"Okay." This was so screwed up. "What do I do?"

"Start a conversation with him. Me. Whatever. And remember—be open and vulnerable." Frankie—ahem,

Teague—picked up his coffee and gazed out at the trees, all stoic and shit.

Open and vulnerable. Right.

Uh, how?

"I really like you."

Frankie's stoic Teague persona dropped away. "Oh my gods, Chris, we're not in high school."

"What? It's the truth! I'm being open and vulnerable, putting myself out there."

"And putting pressure on him at the same time." He turned an ear toward the cabin. "He's up. Why don't you make him breakfast, and I'll get more coffee going?"

"He likes peanut butter, right?"

"I think so."

Great. Then I could do breakfast.

***

Teague hated peanut butter. Because of course he did.

I looked helplessly at the sandwich I'd put together for him after he'd politely declined and headed outside onto the porch, where Frankie was. Their low voices teased the edge of my hearing, Teague sounding far more animated with Frankie than the cold "No, thank you" he'd given me when I'd held out the plate and said, "Peanut butter?"

Okay...maybe my delivery needed a little work.

I leaned against the kitchen counter and shoved a bite of the sandwich into my mouth. Frankie had stolen half my breakfast, so there was no point in letting peanut butter go to waste. As I chewed, I mulled over what Frankie and I had talked about. Open and vulnerable. I wasn't stupid—I understood what he was getting at. Let my walls down. Show Teague my squishy underbelly.

Wait for him to rake stone talons across it.

I finished the sandwich in a couple more bites and sighed. Sitting still and thinking had never been my strength. I needed to be *doing*.

Luckily, I'd gotten pretty good at chopping wood.

Chapter 6

Frankie

One good thing about this tiny, tiny little cabin—there were no pressing chores to distract me from watching Chris swing an axe around.

I sat on the porch, a second mug of coffee warming my hands, my eyes following every bunch and extension of Chris's very impressive muscles. He wielded an axe like he'd been born a lumberjack, and I was here for it. His scent drifted across the yard to tease my senses—clean sweat and a sweet floral note that reminded me of wildflowers growing in mountain pastures. My cat purred in appreciation.

Teague chuckled. "You didn't hear a word I said, did you?"

I hadn't even realized he'd been talking. Heat flushed my cheeks. "I...no. I'm sorry."

"Don't worry about it." He looked over too, his purple gargoyle eyes warmer than usual when he regarded Chris. "The view's a little distracting."

Chris paused and swiped his forearm across his brow. I was pretty sure he hadn't heard us—his focus remained on his task, and I knew him well enough that if he knew he'd captured our attention so thoroughly, he'd play it up. Instead, he set up another log and continued on.

"Do you think...?" Teague's voice drifted off momentarily, and he cleared his throat. "Do you think you might be interested in him?"

Okay, Frankie, perfect opening. Don't fuck this up. "I got the impression you were."

"Oh, uh..." He shifted in his seat. "No. Not like...not like that."

My brows twitched. "Not like what? You're gay, right?"

Lines that hadn't been there a moment ago etched themselves into brackets around Teague's mouth. I wasn't sure what Drew's gargoyle visage had looked like since he'd broken his curse before I'd met the brothers, but Teague's was closer to human than Rian's had been. Rian had looked like a cartoonish rendition of a goblin, with a jutting nose and chin that almost formed a half-moon. Teague's features were more human. Sharper, especially his prominent cheekbones and forehead ridge, but generally the right proportion.

"No, I'm not gay."

His words could've knocked me over with a feather. "You're *straight*?"

"Not straight either." He sighed. "I'm...I think the modern term is asexual?"

Well. That would explain a lot. I hadn't met someone who identified as asexual before—generally, shifters had strong libidos, thanks to our animal sides. Not to say that ace shifters didn't exist. I'm sure they did. But one of the ways Chris and I had known we were mates was the instant, strong sexual attraction between us.

"Asexual." I nodded slowly. "What does that mean for you? I know there's a range."

"You do?"

"Technically, I'm pan, but I'm usually more attracted to male-presenting people than female. I did a lot of reading as I was figuring myself out. Though I ruled out asexual pretty quickly." I shot him a smile.

He returned it, a flash of a grin, before his expression settled into something more serious and uncomfortable. "I'm not used to talking about it."

"You never discussed it with your brothers?"

"I have, though I didn't have the right vocabulary until recently. Back when we first woke, they were mourning their ability to have sex—"

"Wait. The curse makes you not able to have sex?"

"Apparently, they couldn't have sex in their human form. Drew tried, and that was what sent us scrambling for protection and why we entered into the agreement with the MacGrath pack."

"Damn." I let out a low whistle. "So they hadn't had sex for...five hundred years?"

"They hadn't. Not until Drew figured out Josh was his true love and the same for Rian, with Logan."

"Wow. Just...*wow*."

Five hundred years of celibacy. Even if that was broken into twenty-five-year chunks of being awake, the brothers had been going on *one hundred years* without getting their freak on. I couldn't imagine going for a year without. Actually, my longest dry spell had probably been the past few months at the mansion, and my cat was definitely feeling the need to have that itch scratched.

My gaze wandered over to Chris, who was stacking up quite a wood pile. He was still wearing his shirt though. Dammit.

Teague's voice drew my attention back to him. "I've never had sex. Never had any desire to."

"Are you aromantic too?"

"I don't think so?" He shifted in his chair. "Though, hell, I might be. Who knows. That would be the perfect insult to injury, wouldn't it? To have a curse that can only be broken by true love and for me to be incapable of it."

I put my empty mug on the table and shifted in my seat so I was facing him, my knees drawn up to my chest. Chris could take lessons from Teague on being open and vulnerable because, damn, how brave was Teague being in this conversation? He was clearly out of his element but still sharing with me. It took a lot of guts to do that.

"I'm no expert on sexuality," I started, "but I think we can talk through this, maybe help you figure some stuff out. You game?"

Teague scratched the back of his neck, every muscle in his body tense with discomfort. I could scent the emotion rolling off him, and I worked at projecting calmness and encouragement in his direction. Finally, he lowered his hand and gave me a nod. "Sure," he said, a little breathless.

"Are you fulfilled by the friendships and familial relationships you have, or do you want a partner?"

"A partner. Definitely." Though he gave the answer immediately, with no hesitation, he paused right after. "I...I want to love," he continued tentatively. "I see what Drew and Rian found, and I want that for myself. But I don't know if I'm capable of it."

"If you want it, you're capable of it."

"Maybe not, with this soul bond in place."

"What do you mean?"

He looked at me, silent for a second. "How do you think the true-love business happens? Two souls connect.

But Chris already tied mine to his. While that bond's in place, there's no way for my soul to recognize my true love."

My mouth dropped open. Holy shit. No wonder he was so pissed at Chris. "Are you sure?"

"No. This curse didn't come with an instruction manual." He rubbed a hand over his heart. "But...I feel it."

"Did he know—"

Teague was shaking his head before I finished. "He does now, but before he cast it? No. I think if he had, he would've found another way. I like to believe that, anyway."

"I'm sure he would've."

I glanced over at Chris. At some point, he'd removed his shirt, but his bare chest wasn't as captivating as it would have been a few minutes ago. My brain was still trying to untangle the ramifications of the spell he'd imposed on Teague and the fact he'd never fully explained it. Up until now, the casting of the spell had been an academic sort of thing to me. It had happened before I'd met the two of them. Of course I knew of it—it had been explained to me at one point, though I couldn't remember when—but the idea that he'd made breaking Teague's curse impossible while trying to break his own...

"Don't tell Drew or Rian, please."

"They should know."

"If Chris follows through on bringing Keelan up here to undo the spell, they won't have to."

Right. And I'd do my damnedest to make sure he did.

<hr>

As soon as Teague returned to the interior of the cabin to dig up something for lunch for the three of us, I marched across the lawn, meadow, whatever it was, to confront Chris. "We need to talk."

He paused in the midst of wiping his forehead with his discarded shirt, moving it enough to the side that he could meet my eyes. "Uh-oh. What?"

"He can't break his own curse because of you?"

Chris groaned and tossed his shirt back onto the pile of logs he'd recently split. "I didn't know."

"I hope not!"

"Seriously. I didn't." There was nothing but sincerity in his deep-brown eyes, and his expression was somber. "It never occurred to me that it would interfere in any way." He sighed. "It should've though."

"Uh, yeah, damn straight it should've. What the hell, Chris? You need to get Keelan up here, like now."

"Yeah, I'll just summon them through the power of thought." He rolled his eyes.

I smacked his biceps, and though it wasn't my intention, my palm lingered on his arm. His skin was cool, a little damp, but I could feel the heat and power beneath the surface. His scent swirled around me, the floral notes as surprising as always but perfectly Chris. What I wouldn't give to have his arms around me... *Godsdammit, focus, Francisco.* "Don't be an asshole. You've got a truck—go into Clearwater and call them."

"Now?"

"Now."

He frowned. "You're awfully bossy for such a small guy."

I glared as I put both hands on my hips, ready for a confrontation I should've known was coming. Everyone saw me and thought *pretty, delicate,* and therefore *submissive,* and fuck that. I was done hiding behind a façade in order to keep myself and the ones I cared about safe. "You got a problem with it? Because I'm not changing for any—"

He placed a finger over my lips. I was tempted to bite it, but I didn't. Instead, I strengthened my glare.

"It was an observation, nothing more," he said softly, withdrawing his finger. "Not a judgment or a complaint."

"Sounded like a complaint," I muttered.

"I promise it wasn't." He offered a tentative smile, then reached for his shirt. "I can head to Clearwater, no problem. You're right. I should get Keelan up here as soon as possible. We need to get this done."

Now that Chris was covered again, I sort of mourned the loss of his bare chest. I hadn't even had a chance to properly appreciate it, and my cat was not happy about that. He yowled softly in my head, annoyed with the decisions his human half was making—which, honestly, was the situation about ninety percent of the time. He was a hard beast to please.

"Also, I found out something about Teague."

"Hm?"

"He's ace."

Chris's brows twitched. "That's...asexual, right?"

"Right. And he's sex-averse."

"Which means...?"

"He doesn't want sex. Never had it, never wanted it, still doesn't."

His eyes widened. "Like, never?"

"Never."

"Oh shit." His eyes widened further as the implications set in. "I don't...how do we...?"

I knew where the sputtering came from because that *OMG, what do we do* worry was the same thing I was feeling. Seducing someone, finding intimacy through sex...I mean, I'd done it. I hadn't found love that way, but I'd found companionship and fun. I'd never approached a potential partner from a friendship angle first, and I certainly had never done so without the end goal of sex in mind. So how was I—were we—going to convince Teague he was our mate? Because he was, I felt that in the core of my being. My cat was certain, and I always listened to him. At least, when it counted.

"He wants a partner. He wants to love." My glare returned. "Which is why you need to get rid of the goddamned soul bond so his soul can recognize ours."

"Right. Step one." He scrubbed a hand through the hair on top of his head, making it stand up every which way. He didn't notice—he never did. "Step two will be figuring out... what do they call it? Teague's love language."

My brows rose in surprise. "You know about love languages?"

Was it my imagination, or was there a slight blush coloring Chris's cheeks? "I, uh, might have done some reading on it."

"Why?" I drew out the question, a sly smile on my lips.

"It was back before I met him in person, before I even came up with the stupid idea of Keelan's spell." Another scrub through his hair. "I thought maybe I would...woo him."

I rolled my eyes. "You should've stuck with that plan."

"Gods, you're not kidding." He huffed out a breath. "Okay, I'll be back in a few hours. Don't get into trouble while I'm gone."

I popped up on my tiptoes and kissed his cheek. "No promises."

Chapter 7

Teague

Frankie reentered the cabin as the engine of Chris's truck turned over. I paused in putting sandwiches together to watch the beaten old vehicle head down the drive.

"He gave up already?" I shook my head, returning to the task at hand. "It hasn't even been twenty-four hours."

Frankie closed the space between us, and I nearly jumped when his hand came to rest on my back. The contact intensified his emotions for a second until I was able to shore up my mental walls, but it was enough to get a quick flash of anger, concern, contentment, and frustration. That was the thing about emotions—people rarely felt only one thing at a time. Usually, it was a mix of strong primary feelings paired with secondary and tertiary emotions, and parsing them all out often took more effort than I was willing to expend. This ability of mine was an invasion of privacy. Occasionally useful, yes, but unlike Drew's control over metal and Rian's growing proficiency with runes, I couldn't *not* use my empathy. It was always there, always on, and the best I could do was ignore it or tune it out.

"He's heading to Clearwater to call Keelan and arrange for them to come do the ritual here. As he promised." The last was said with a bit of reproach in his voice, and sure, I deserved it. It was hard not to think the worst of Chris after...everything.

"I thought half a day without an indoor toilet had done him in."

"Big, burly wolf-bear, and he can't handle roughing it." Frankie grinned. "Not like you and me."

"I'm not sure that's a comment on our characters or more about our backgrounds."

"Let's go with the former. If only so we can rub it in." Frankie chuckled. "Need a hand?"

I shook my head and presented him with a camp plate bearing a roast beef sandwich made with the cold cuts and bread we'd picked up in Clearwater the day before. There wasn't much to it—we'd forgotten to get lettuce or other vegetables that would go on a sandwich. Our fresh produce haul consisted of a bag of potatoes and some bananas. If I'd known Chris was heading back to town, I would've asked him to pick up some tomatoes or something. Rude of him to go without checking in.

My lips screwed into a disapproving line, and I said, "Eat up. I guess we can split the one I made for Chris if you're still hungry after that."

Frankie eyed me as he took the plate. "What's that sour look for?"

I hesitated, then let out a breath. "Chris. He couldn't have asked if we wanted him to get anything?"

Frankie sat at the questionable dining table, giving it a test push and discovering it was surprisingly steady. He set his plate on it and waved imperiously for me to sit across from him.

"I told him to go," Frankie said before sinking his teeth into the sandwich. Once he was finished chewing, he continued, "And I didn't think to suggest he stop at the store for anything."

"But he could've—"

"Teague." Frankie laid his forearms on the table and leaned closer. "I don't know if you've noticed, but Chris is not the most...aware man on the planet."

I rolled my eyes. "You don't say."

"You've got to start giving him a break."

I wanted to argue that. I didn't have to do anything—I was the wronged party, not him. I was the one who'd had a spell cast on him without his consent. At least, I hadn't consented to the spell that was actually cast, only the one that I thought was being cast.

Frankie worked his way through his sandwich, a contemplative look on his face as though he were figuring out how he wanted to say something. I was tempted to let the leash off my senses to get an idea of what he was feeling as he worked through whatever it was in his head, but I didn't. Instead, I focused on eating. The sandwich was adequate to fuel my body, but it might as well have been made of sawdust for all I tasted it.

Frankie finished the last of his sandwich and reached for half of the one I'd made for Chris. Pausing, he met my gaze, his expression somber. "Before Drew and Rian found Josh and Logan, if you'd seen a chance to break your curse for all of you that didn't involve finding your true loves, would you have taken it?"

Well, *that* was a loaded question. "Depends on what the chance was."

"Let's assume it was an option that wouldn't result in anyone's injury or death."

"Strings?"

"None you can see."

"Yes." If no one would be hurt, a thousand times yes. This curse was all because of me. I would have jumped at the opportunity to undo it.

Frankie nodded as though my answer was a given. He knew me well enough by now that he likely hadn't expected anything else. "How is that any different from what Chris did?"

I opened my mouth...then closed it. How indeed? Although I'd said only a short time ago that I didn't think Chris had taken the action he had with malice in his heart, I'd been acting as though he had, hadn't I? The deception was wrong, there was no arguing that, but Frankie's point was valid. If I'd been in Chris's situation and looking to save my family, would I have let morals get in my way?

Still, I was angry. I'd known from the very beginning that finding someone who could love me and break my curse was all but impossible. But after seeing Drew and Rian find their true loves, part of me had hoped. Hoped desperately. And for that hope to be quashed by Chris's actions...

Could I forgive him?

I pondered that question for the rest of the afternoon as Frankie and I stacked the wood Chris had cut. Then Frankie found a relatively dry area of the yard at the same time a sunbeam did, and suddenly I was sharing space with a giant mountain lion intent on soaking up as much sun as he could. I retreated to the porch, which was, lamentably, not in the sun, and spent an unknown amount of time watching Frankie's tail and ears twitch as he instinctively categorized every sound in the surrounding forest.

It was...surprisingly calming. I couldn't remember the

last time I'd simply sat and done nothing for any length of time. Back home, if I wasn't on duty, there were always things to do around the mansion. Helping Drew with his latest project, for instance, mostly for a chance to bond over working together rather than any innate talent I had with engines. Or sitting for Rian to etch a rune into my skin on the off chance it would actually get us a step closer to breaking the curse without true love—though I wasn't a fan of the feeling of the tattoo needle, so Drew was more frequently his test subject. There were yard chores, cleaning inside, or running over to Josh's parents' house to help them with something—a tiny bit of thanks for all the years they'd looked after us before Josh took over. In short, there was always something.

But here...here I could just be.

I must have dozed off because the next thing I knew, my eyes jolted open at the sound of a truck making its way down the rutted, bumpy drive to the cabin. I blinked the sleep out of my eyes as Chris's battered pickup came into view, going faster than he should be on the muddy path masquerading as a laneway. He hit the brakes hard and slid a foot on the brown grass to a complete stop.

I sat straighter as his emotions reached me. Frustration, anger, worry. Of course I didn't need my ability to recognize those emotions, given how he jerked the door open and jumped out, every one of his movements abrupt.

"They're gone." Thanks to his curse, his eyes glowed a muted orange instead of the bright hue of a rageful shifter. "Of all the fucking times—"

He went to kick at the front tire of his truck, but Frankie was suddenly there in his human skin, shirtless, his pants slightly askew. One of his hipbones peeked above the waistband, and I had no business admiring that delicate curve with its intricate shadows. He pushed Chris back, and Chris stumbled but made no further attempt to kick anything.

"You'll hurt yourself," Frankie scolded. "Calm down. Who's gone?"

Chris raked a hand through his hair as I trotted down the steps to join them next to the truck. "Keelan," he growled. "They told my sister they needed to leave, and... they left. Without a single fucking clue as to where or why or anything."

My stomach sank. "You've got their number, though, right?"

"*The number you are trying to reach is no longer in service,*" Chris said mockingly. "How could they—they were supposed to be my friend, dammit."

A boulder lodged itself in my throat. That was that then. No finding my true love. No breaking my curse. Unless Keelan reappeared sometime in the next year or so— and I didn't end up in jail because of Muirloch's lies—I would sleep in stone once more.

And when I awoke, I would be well and truly alone.

Chapter 8

Chris

I swore to all the gods that if Keelan appeared in front of me right now, I'd wring their neck. Then hug them. And then beg them to do the unbonding as they'd promised.

As angry as I was with them, I was more worried. It wasn't like them to disappear without letting me know in advance. They'd gone off on sabbaticals before—alone time where they could meditate or do whatever they needed to do to keep their magic running freely—but never without word of where they were going and when they'd be back. And certainly never with canceling their phone. They were a part of my family, and I knew they cared for us as much as we cared for them.

So something had to have driven them away. Could it be Muirloch?

I was too restless to stay in the cabin. Out in the woods, I leaned against a tree in the darkness and cast my eyes skyward, straining to glimpse the moon through the canopy of pine boughs. It was full tonight, and no doubt, if I were a true werewolf, I'd feel the pull of it and be frolicking around in my wolf form. As it was, I was a bear at heart, with no ties to the moon, and I felt no urge to pull on my fur. Shifting wasn't the joy I remembered it being when I was a teenager before my stupid father went and got himself killed and his family cursed. Instead, shifting was a chore and a constant reminder that I was *wrong*.

A slight rustle nearby alerted me to the fact I was no longer alone. Frankie's minty, spicy scent tickled my nose, but I didn't turn in his direction, knowing I wouldn't be able to see him anyway. Goddamn my cursed senses.

"Couldn't sleep?" The question was soft, barely louder than his footsteps on the moist earth.

"No. Worried."

He leaned against the same tree I was, his shoulder brushing my elbow. "Of course. Do you think they had a family emergency or something?"

I shrugged. "Honestly, I don't know much about Keelan. Going through every time I've tried to find out more about them, I've realized they've been cagey, dodging my questions and not sharing much at all, and distracting me from asking more. I considered them my friend, but...I'm beginning to think it wasn't reciprocated."

"I'm sorry, Chris."

"Me too." It hurt more than I thought it should, but I'd trusted Keelan, dammit. I cleared my throat, dislodging the lump that had suddenly shown up.

Frankie's fingers drifted across my ear and upward, softly threading through my messy hair. "I wish I could fix it for you."

I leaned into his touch, a low rumble escaping me as his fingers pressed into my scalp more firmly. His nails scratched the skin just right, and I all but melted in his direction. Our lips meeting wasn't a conscious decision, the same as on New Year's Eve. Then, we'd been sitting outside, talking, away from the music and loud conversation of the rest of the group that had been there for the party. Though we hadn't said the words to each other, we both knew who the other one was to us—mates—and that tension had hummed between us the entire night. But the third piece of us had been missing. Still was.

I braced a hand on the bark above Frankie's head as I pressed him into the tree trunk, devouring him. His lips were pliant against mine, eager, opening to invite me in. My tongue touched his, a brief, teasing swipe, and I nearly drowned in his taste. His scent. It enveloped me, crisp mint and spice. If I could hear my bear, no doubt he'd be rumbling in appreciation. But he was as silent as he'd been for thirty years.

Gods, it was so tempting to just *take*, especially with Frankie pushing up on his toes, so eager for the kiss to continue. It would be effortless to strip him down and fuck him—no penetration since I didn't have lube, but spit and precome would go a long way to easing friction if we rutted together. Except...

I pulled back with a gasp and laid my forehead against Frankie's. "We can't."

Frankie mewled in protest, but then he gave a tiny shake of his head. "I know. You're right. But damn, Chris. I want you."

Those low words, with more than a little bit of his cat in his voice, almost made me say *fuck it* and go with the plan of frotting on the forest floor. Reluctantly, I stepped back, putting a foot of space between us. The way his eyes glowed orange briefly, I could tell his cat wasn't pleased. But it was rare that Frankie let his inner animal control him, and now was no exception.

"We need a plan. A serious plan. Getting rid of the bond is out, but..." Frankie trailed off. "Wait. If you're bonded to Teague, how is your soul recognizing me as your—well, one of your mates?"

My eyes widened. Good question. "I hadn't thought of that, and I didn't get a chance to ask Keelan. I never told them about you."

"Oh, they knew. I could see it when they looked at me."

"So maybe Teague's got it all wrong?" My heart leaped with hope. If he was wrong, then we didn't need to dissolve the bond first, which meant Keelan disappearing wasn't the disaster I'd first thought...at least, not for the reasons I'd thought. Still a disaster, only another sort of disaster.

"Maybe." Frankie pursed his lips. "Unless the mate bond works differently than Teague's true-love thing." He waved a hand. "All your curses need to come with instruction manuals, godsdammit."

Despite the topic, I chuckled. "If I could pull one out of my ass for you, I would."

"Ew."

I laughed harder at Frankie's disgusted face. "Well, since that's not happening, let's talk about a plan."

OPERATION: Woo Teague started the next morning. Or, well, later that morning. When the sun was up. I'd wanted to give the plan a much cooler name—something like Purple Sunrise because of the color of Teague's eyes—but Frankie wasn't really on board with the whole naming thing to start with, so I'd kept it simple.

We'd ended up on the forest floor after all, but sitting,

not fucking. Over the wee hours of the morning, we plotted out how we would convince Teague he was ours.

Step one: show Teague I was sorry for lying to him instead of saying it.

Thank gods Frankie had ideas of how to go about that because I didn't. Especially not out here in the wilderness. Frankie had dismissed my idea of picking up a bouquet of flowers for Teague. *Cliché*, he'd said. *Overdone and meaningless.* And...okay, I could see his point. But it was a classic go-to for a reason, wasn't it? I'd suggested I get a giant bouquet, so large I'd have difficulty bringing it back to the cabin in my truck.

Frankie had squinted at me in that doubtful way and simply said, "No."

Which was why I was now in the woods, hunting down a deer. By myself. In my fur. Bears rarely hunted much of anything, and wolves hunted in packs, so I wasn't sure what Frankie expected me to accomplish on my own.

This was not going to end well.

***

It was midafternoon when I trudged out of the woods, naked, holding my trophy. Every muscle in my body ached, I was covered in dirt and leaves from head to toe, and I was pretty sure I had bruises where there should never be bruises, thanks to slipping on some wet rocks on the bank of a stream that was so cold it should've been frozen solid. But I was successful.

Kind of.

Teague saw me first. He was sitting on the porch, in his usual spot, wearing athletic pants and a long-sleeved shirt over his living stone skin. He popped out of his seat and down the cabin steps, his purple eyes flaring. "Where the hell have you been?"

Well, that wasn't the greeting I'd expected. Sure, he might not know I'd gone hunting for him, but still. After the trials of my hunt, on top of a sleepless night, I was done. I thrust my hard-fought trophy at him. "Here."

He didn't have any choice but to accept it, fumbling until he got a good grip. "Is this...a rabbit?"

"The fucker nearly gouged my eye out, so you better fucking appreciate it."

Teague looked at the bundle of fur, then peered at my face, looking for the injury. It had stopped bleeding, but the scratches pulled whenever I moved my facial muscles, so I knew they hadn't healed yet. Stupid curse.

"Why would you think I wanted you to hunt down a rabbit?"

"I was going for a deer, but I only found one, and the damn thing kicked at my head before I could even get close, so I figured a rabbit was a better choice." I rolled my eyes—dumb move because hadn't I just been thinking about how the scratches hurt? "Rabbits are mean assholes."

"O-oh."

I couldn't make heads or tails of Teague's expression. His lips were pinched, and there were crinkles at the edges of his eyes, but I wasn't sure if it was in displeasure or disbelief or...I didn't know, something else entirely. I was too tired to figure it out. "So there. I hunted down supper for you to show you I'm sorry."

"That's why?"

"Why else would I do it?"

"To be honest, Chris, I have no idea."

I grunted. "Now you know. There's your supper. Please

forgive me for being an asshole with the spell. I'm going to bed."

I don't know what possessed me, maybe the fact I was so damned tired I could barely see straight, but I reached out to cup his cheek. It was a quick gesture, but the feel of my skin against his was almost enough to revive me. Almost. My hand dropped away as I groaned.

I was shocked when Teague grabbed it and squeezed. "Thank you."

Even though Teague's touch was there and gone a breath later, the gesture broke through the fog of fatigue around me. "You're welcome."

He cleared his throat and kept his eyes on the rabbit as he said, "Go wash up. You don't want those scratches to get infected."

I took the admonishment for what it was—progress. The roughly spoken words buoyed me through a quick scrub with ice-cold water from the well until I tumbled onto the couch. I was out before my head hit the pillow.

Chapter 9

Frankie

Every time I thought of the rabbit stew simmering on the camp stove, I wanted to giggle.

It was totally unfair, and I knew it, but I never said I didn't have my own asshole tendencies. It was just... Chris was this big, masculine guy with muscles on his muscles, and the best he could bring down was a rabbit. A rabbit that had nearly gotten the best of him, no less.

"I see that look," Teague admonished me as he stepped onto the porch holding an unopened can of beer. He'd gone in to check on Chris, who was passed out on the couch, dead to the world. "Don't make fun of him."

It warmed my heart to hear Teague defending the man he'd been angry at for so long. "I'm not. I promise."

"Your face says otherwise."

I couldn't keep my grin from widening. "Okay, but...a rabbit. A single rabbit."

"You think you could do better?"

"Pfft. I know I could. But this isn't a competition. The point was to—" I broke off, realizing too late that I'd given myself away.

"Pray tell. What was the point?" Teague arched an eyebrow. "Did you plot this together?"

I swallowed, not wanting to get into the broader implications without Chris present. "He wanted to show you he was truly sorry."

"By hunting for me."

"I suggested a deer."

"If he almost got taken out by a rabbit, I'm glad he didn't make more of an effort to get a deer." Teague's lips twitched. "Is this a shifter thing? Apology via wild game?"

It was a mate thing, but I wasn't getting into that. "It's the most basic of gestures, don't you think? Sustenance provided through hard work."

"Very hard work." Teague's grin broke free. "I shouldn't find this so amusing."

I returned his smile. "Why not? I do." As Teague claimed his usual seat, I leaned closer and lowered my voice. "Between us, Chris isn't a very good shifter."

"Because of the curse?"

I shook my head, still smiling. "No, because he's Chris. I mean, come on, a shifter who balks at an outhouse?"

"To be fair, I'm not fond of the outhouse either."

"But you don't whine about it."

He shook his head and held out the can of beer. "Would you mind? I can get one for you too, but I thought you were still working on your tea."

I popped the tab on the beer for him, knowing it was impossible for him to do so with his talons, and handed it back. "There you go. I'm good with the tea, thanks."

Silence fell, but it was comfortable. No tension between us, simply two friends enjoying each other's presence. Beyond the porch, snow fell, first in gently drifting flakes, then more heavily. The day had been gloomy, but now it turned downright dark, even though it was only slightly past four in the afternoon. I cast a worried glance at the sky, what I could see through the trees. The clouds smelled heavy with snow, but there was something else...

A sudden *boom* made me jump. It didn't help that I knew exactly what it was—thunder—my entire body shook like the boughs on the surrounding pine trees under the onslaught of the gusting wind. Then, instead of rain pouring down, it began snowing.

"Huh." Teague edged closer to the porch railing so he could look directly upward at the sky. "Thundersnow?"

Okay, Francisco. Calm down. This is not a full-blown storm. That's probably the only crack of thunder in it. I took a deep breath and let it out slowly, tamping down the jitters in my chest and stomach so they wouldn't be obvious in my voice. "I guess? Maybe we should go ins—"

Boom.

I couldn't help the cry that escaped as I curled tighter on the chair. In an instant, Teague was kneeling in front of me, his hands not hesitating to touch me for once. They'd landed on the sides of my thighs, holding tight, his talons barely there pinpricks through the material of my sweatpants.

"Frankie? Sweetheart, talk to me. What's wrong?"

"Th-thunder." I didn't look at him. I couldn't. I was twenty-five fucking years old, and I was scared of thunder. No, not simply scared—petrified. I wanted nothing more than to uncurl, relax, laugh off my reaction, but irrational reactions were just that. Irrational. Uncontrollable.

"Okay. Okay. Let's get you inside."

I didn't protest as Teague awkwardly lifted me into his arms, especially since there was another crack of thunder. I threw my arms around his neck and buried my face against his cooler-than-normal skin. In this form, his skin felt thicker than my human skin, tougher, but still soft and supple. Comforting.

A long rumble from the sky chased us inside, almost as though the storm was annoyed I'd escaped it.

"Wha's goin' on?" Chris slurred from the couch. I peeked under my arm to find him sitting up, creases marking one cheek. He rubbed his eyes and opened them wide, likely in an effort to wake up fully. "I thought I heard thunder."

On cue, thunder cracked louder than the previous ones. I made an *eep* noise and tucked my head against Teague's skin again. My safe place.

"Thundersnow," Teague said.

"Seriously? That's weird."

Teague grunted. "You want to scoot over?"

"Oh yeah, sure."

There was rustling, and then Teague was sitting. He made no attempt to dislodge me, and I wasn't ready to let go. This was as close to Teague as I'd ever been. Physically, maybe emotionally too. Not that I could truly appreciate it at the moment, with my insides trying to shake themselves loose.

A hand stroked my back. Not Teague's—there was no hint of talons. "It's okay," Chris murmured. "It's only thunder."

"He's not stupid. He knows it's just thunder."

"I'm trying to help."

"Maybe don't treat him like a child then?"

"S-stop," I managed. "You're b-both being idiots."

"Sorry, sweetheart," Teague said immediately.

"Sorry," Chris echoed. "How are you doing?"

The contact from my two men—even if one didn't know

he was mine yet—was helping. It kept me grounded instead of letting me get all twisted up in my head, which was what usually happened when I huddled under blankets during a storm. Memories and childhood associations with thunder took me by surprise every time. But for right now, Teague's and Chris's touch kept that all at bay.

"Okay." Not the total truth, but not a lie either. Until thunder flared again, and I shrank into a ball.

Chris moved closer, and Teague shifted so the larger man wouldn't sit on his legs. I let out a shaky sigh as Chris pressed fully against my back. Suddenly I was a Frankie sandwich, and I couldn't complain about that. I let out a soft, shaky sigh and melted into the embrace.

I wasn't sure how long we sat like that. It was well after the thunder stopped. Well after true dark fell too. None of us seemed eager to end the connection we'd forged during the storm, least of all me. I felt delicate and breakable like I always did after one of these episodes, but the difference this time was that I wasn't alone.

At some point, we'd all moved so we were lying down —no longer a sandwich, more of a puppy pile. Teague made a surprisingly comfortable mattress and Chris a heavy but wonderful blanket. I didn't generally go for all this closeness, but for these two guys, I'd make an exception.

"Are you...are you *purring?*" Chris suddenly demanded.

"No," I lied.

"He's been purring for the past fifteen minutes," Teague countered with a chuckle. "You're only feeling it now?"

"I thought maybe he had phlegm in his chest or something. I was about to whack his back to see if he'd cough it up."

I laughed silently, not quite ready to make much more

noise than my purring—stupid cat—in the quiet cocoon of the cabin. "Thank you for not whacking me."

"You're welcome," Chris said seriously.

Another rumble sounded—not the thunder or my purring this time, but Chris's stomach. My eyes flew wide. "Oh shit. The stew."

I went to get up, but Chris's firm hand prevented me. "It's fine. I'll get it."

Falling back against Teague's chest, I moaned. "Fuck, Chris. I'm sorry. It's probably burned by now."

"You had it on low, so maybe not," Teague said.

On low, yeah, but I hadn't stirred it for how long now? Ugh, if I'd ruined Chris's apology rabbit, I was going to be mad at myself. All because of a little thunder. I sat up and tugged on my hair. "I'm so *stupid.*"

"Hey, no, none of that." Teague scooted upward as well and grabbed my chin gently in his taloned fingers to make me look at him. I resisted for only a second. "You're not stupid. I don't know what's at the root of your fear of thunder, but whatever it is, it's not stupid."

"Teague, I'm a fucking adult. I shouldn't be cowering like a child when there are loud noises in the sky."

"Rationally, sure. But I'm willing to bet that when that first crack of thunder happens, every bit of rationality flees your brain, doesn't it?"

I pressed my lips together and swept my hair over one shoulder. He wasn't wrong, but I wasn't about to admit it aloud.

"Stew's fine!" Chris called as he kicked the door open with a foot, a little stronger than necessary. The door hit the wall with a *crack,* and I jumped, still sensitive to loud noises.

"Críost. You're a bull in a china shop. You didn't break

the door, did you?" Teague got up to examine it. Apparently, it was fine because he closed it with a grunt.

"I didn't break the door," Chris grumbled. "Here, come eat."

I watched the two interact with a growing warmth in my heart. The animosity that had been there every time Teague looked at Chris was gone. Instead of being filled with venom, as they had been as recently as our arrival at the cabin, Teague's words were missing heat. The bickering was just that—bickering like an old married couple might partake in.

It gave me hope that Teague's heart was opening up again to Chris.

"Frankie, get your cute butt over here." Chris held up a bowl for me and his eyes widened as he realized what he'd said.

"It is a cute butt, isn't it?" Teague smiled at me, his purple eyes sparkling, and I let out a silent breath of relief.

Tension left Chris's expression. "The cutest. Come on, before it gets cold."

For the first time, we all sat around the tiny but surprisingly sturdy table, Chris on one side and Teague and I on the other. We couldn't sit directly across from each other—the table was too narrow for two bowls side-by-side—so Chris sat between us.

At the first taste of the stew, Chris looked surprised. "Hey, this is pretty good."

I gave him a wry look. "Thanks so much for your confidence in my cooking."

Immediately, his cheeks pinkened. "No, I mean—sorry. I meant the seasoning and whatever is decent."

"You're wounding him with faint praise," Teague said.

There was a curl to the corner of his lips that gave away his amusement.

"I'm what?"

"You're giving me backward compliments," I clarified.

"No! What? No." Chris shook his head and blew out a breath. "Okay, no, I meant I'm surprised but *happy* you found enough spices and shit in the cabin to make the stew tasty. I didn't expect that." He cast an apologetic look at me. "Better?"

"Marginally," Teague said. "Better would have been, 'Thank you for taking my scrawny apology rabbit and turning it into delicious stew, Frankie. You're the best.'"

"Thank you for taking my *amazingly plump and juicy*" —Chris glared at Teague—"apology rabbit and turning it into delicious stew, Frankie. You *are* the best."

Grinning, I shook my head at their antics. "It would've been better with two."

Chris threw up his hands in defeat.

"Did you want to talk about earlier?" Teague ventured, his voice soft. Like he was talking to a wounded animal.

I supposed that, in a way, he was. "It won't help."

"You sure?" Chris asked. "You ever talked with anyone about it before?"

I opened my mouth to say *yes*, but then I closed it. Had I? Usually, I was out of sight, and therefore, out of mind during storms. Especially when I was part of Becker's pride. That sort of weakness would have been exploited had I shown it. I didn't think I'd even shared it with Nikki and Sarah, who would have been eminently supportive.

So...yeah. Maybe I should try talking about it.

I left my spoon in my half-empty bowl and swallowed hard. Where to start? "I told you my mom died when I was ten, right?"

Teague nodded, but Chris didn't.

"Sorry," I said to him. "Yeah, she died when I was ten. Until then, it'd been only me and her and whatever pride she happened to affiliate herself with, until another 'better' opportunity came along. That usually meant a new man, and she didn't make the best choices in partners."

"There can't be that many prides in BC though." Chris frowned.

"We went all over Canada and into the States too. Wherever her hunt for a man took us." I sighed. "That makes her sound terrible. She wasn't—she truly loved me. I never once doubted that.

"We were in Ontario when I was ten, somewhere north of Toronto, I think. I can't remember for sure—I didn't pay attention to stuff like that. One night, it was storming, really bad. Huge cracks of thunder, lots of lightning, the works. There was some concern there might be a tornado too.

"Mom was out with her latest man and was late getting home. I started getting worried, and it seemed every new crack of thunder jacked up my anxiety. Then there was a knock on the door, and a cop was there to tell us there'd been an accident. I guess they'd parked to get some privacy, and a tree fell on the guy's car." I rubbed a hand over my face. "I don't even remember his name. Isn't that awful?"

Teague covered one of my hands with his, and after a second, Chris grabbed my other one.

"Not awful," Teague said.

"You were just a kid," Chris added. "And a traumatized one at that."

"My brain associated thunder with losing my mom. For a long time—" I hesitated because it was so ludicrous, I cringed, but...vulnerable and open is the advice I'd given Chris, and I couldn't not follow it myself. "For a long time, I thought the thunder had killed my mom and would kill me next. Like it was a sentient thing that was looking for me."

"You were *ten*." Chris's expression was soft as he reiterated the point. "What happened after you lost your mom?"

"One of the aunties in the pride looked after me for about six months, I want to say. Then she moved to another pride out east but didn't take me with her."

"What?" Teague was offended on my behalf. "Why not?"

"I never really knew. I'd thought she liked me, but maybe she was tired of looking after someone else's kid." I shrugged. "The pride leader worked out something with another pride in southern Alberta and sent me there. I lived with that pride for three or four years, then they moved me to another one, where I stayed for about a year, then back to the southern Alberta pride for another two. When I turned eighteen, I left and ended up with the pride in Prince George, which was a good one until Becker came along and ruined it." I frowned at that memory but comforted myself with the fact that Becker was no longer alive and I had been the one to end his life. Get my revenge. But...yeah, I wasn't ready to be *that* open. Maybe someday, but not today. "Anyway, BC is much better for thunderstorms than Ontario. So you won't have to see me being a coward too often."

"Stop." Teague's voice was harsher than I was used to hearing it. "You're not a coward for reacting to childhood trauma in a totally understandable way, and you're not stupid either. You need to give yourself a break, Frankie."

"I—"

"He's right. Listen to him," Chris said. His voice wasn't as harsh as Teague's, but it was definitely firm. "Your reaction isn't wrong or bad or anything like that. It's completely, totally understandable. The only thing that would be wrong

was if you decided to ride out the next storm alone. I'm—"
He glanced at Teague, who nodded. "*We're* here for you.
Whatever you need."

It said something about my fragile emotional state that
my eyes pricked with tears at that declaration. Had anyone
ever vowed to be there for me other than my mom? And
though she hadn't meant to, she'd broken that vow. I tried to
speak, but I couldn't force any sounds out of my mouth for a
second. Clearing my throat, I tried again.

"Thanks." It was gravelly and barely audible, but I
managed, and I made sure I was thinking hard about my
gratitude so Teague would feel the truth of it.

He grunted in acknowledgment, his purple eyes as soft
as I'd ever seen them. "Eat."

The gruff order was about as close to a declaration of
care as I'd get from him. Yet, anyway. Maybe soon there
would be actual words we could exchange.

All three of us.

Chapter 10

Teague

I parked Chris's truck at the back of the grocery store lot and pulled out my cell phone. It had chirped incessantly since I'd entered an area with service, so I knew I had many messages, but I was still shocked to see double-digit notifications on all my means of contact. It was more than a little weird to be looking at my phone after days of it being turned off and useless, but I quickly fell back into the routine of checking my email, texts, and voicemail. The latter was full, with messages from Gale, my partner on the force, sharing gossip and news she thought I'd be interested in—pretty much the same as she would do during our breaks while on patrol. Shockingly, there was also a message from my commanding officer, giving his support despite the video evidence, and a few other voicemails from colleagues I hadn't expected to hear from, all letting me know they were thinking of me and believed in me.

It went a long way to making me feel like I wasn't completely abandoned by my fellow officers.

Next, I checked my emails. There were a few from Gage, keeping me apprised of his activities on my case. He was doing research and filing things, though I didn't understand half of what he was talking about. The rest were marketing ads from stores I'd foolishly given my contact info. Delete, delete, delete. I wasn't in the mindset to consider new jeans, thanks.

Text messages were last and the most numerous. There were notes from Drew, Josh, and Rian, all inconsequential since they knew I wouldn't be able to respond easily or quickly. Updates about their days, a couple of really bad jokes from Drew he knew I'd appreciate, and a funny story from Josh about taking Logan to the spa owned by Josh's best friend and her brother. Apparently, the brother—Haider—was aghast at the shape of Logan's nails after having a manicure and pedicure only a few short weeks ago. Of course, Haider didn't know that Logan spent part of his time as a wolf, which tended to be hard on one's hands and feet. Instead, he tried to guess all the reasons Logan's nails might be so ragged, each idea crazier than the last—including the idea that Logan was actually a sasquatch in disguise. I chuckled at the tale and wished Josh had been able to tell it to me in person.

Gods, I missed my family.

Bringing up Drew's number, I pressed the button to call him. It rang only once before Drew picked up with an enthusiastic, "Teague!"

It warmed my heart. Stupidly, I'd feared that with me out of sight, my brothers would simply go on with their lives and their loves without giving me another thought. Hearing the warmth in Drew's voice, even if I couldn't feel it because of the physical distance between us, went a long way to assuaging that worry.

"Hello, dearthái r," I said.

"Gods, it's good to hear your voice. Hold on a second.

I'll get Rian." In the background, I heard the patio door open, and then Drew bellowed, "Rian! Teague's on the phone!"

I winced at the volume, but I couldn't keep a wide smile from stretching my lips. No doubt Rian was in the guesthouse with Logan—they'd adopted that as their home since Logan liked having his own den. Drew was being Drew, loud and unapologetic.

"How are you doing?" Drew asked as the patio door closed again. "Have you killed Chris yet?"

"No."

"If you do, we'll come help bury the body."

I laughed at the dark humor. "I don't think that will come to pass, but thank you."

In fact, I hadn't thought of Chris with any sort of animosity for a couple of days now. Ever since the apology rabbit. I supposed it'd done what it was supposed to, but it was more than the rabbit turning my head when it came to Chris. It was the way he had clearly gone out of his comfort zone to do it. Or, to be honest, the adorable fact he was a shifter who preferred civilization to the woods. I'd already known he wasn't perfect—*gods*, I had known—but those characteristics made him all the more human.

"Did I miss him?" Rian sounded a little out of breath as the patio door slammed shut behind him.

"No, he's still on the line. You're on speaker now, Teague."

"Hey, Rian."

"Teague." There was relief in Rian's voice, and it confirmed my brothers were missing me as much as I was missing them. "It's great to hear from you. How's it going?"

"He hasn't killed Chris yet," Drew informed him.

"Bonus points for good behavior then." Rian laughed. "I

was surprised he insisted on going with you. Frankie, not so much."

"Really? Why's that?"

Rian paused. "You're kidding, right?"

"I...no?"

"You're such an oblivious sod sometimes." I could practically hear Drew rolling his eyes. "He likes you, Teague. A lot."

Immediately, I scoffed. "No."

"Yes."

"Scut. No, there's no way."

"Grow some eyes, man," Rian said, laughing. "We've all seen the way he looks at you. Even Logan's commented on it."

I opened my mouth, then closed it, flustered. "He's... he's way too young."

"Gods. He's about Josh's age."

"Younger," I corrected.

"But close to," Rian countered. "Besides, *everyone* is young compared to us, Teague. Even if you only count the years we were awake, we're all pushing a century and a half."

"Yes, true, but—"

"What's your next excuse?" Drew cut in, a hint of laughter in his voice. "Let's hear it."

I bristled at the idea that he was finding this humorous. "You know it's not as easy for me as it—"

"If you suggest in your next breath that finding someone was easy for Drew and me," Rian all but growled, "I'll come up there and smack you upside the head."

I huffed out a breath. "You're right. I'm sorry."

"Look," he continued, his voice softer, "it has to be hard to shake the idea that there's something wrong with you, but there isn't. You're built differently, and that's okay. Being asexual isn't a flaw."

"I know." Even if it made me feel so very odd when compared to my brothers.

"Do you?" Drew challenged. "Because it seems to me like you're still in the mindset that you'll never break the curse because you don't want to have sex with anyone."

Sometimes I regretted being open with my brothers, but when it'd been the three of us against the world, it was hard not to be. "In this day and age, where everything is so sexualized, who would want to love me without sex?"

In some ways, it might have been easier back in our natural lifetime for me to find a partner. It probably would have been a woman, given the expectations of the church and the need to produce heirs, but perhaps I would have been able to lie with her to fulfill that duty at least once. But now, people wanted sex as recreation, for fun, and I...didn't.

"How's the cabin?" Drew's change of topic was quite welcome, and we spent the next few minutes discussing the ruggedness of the place, along with Chris's lack of appreciation of it. Of course I had to share the story of the apology rabbit, which had both of my brothers in stitches by the time I was done.

When I signed off fifteen minutes later, with the promise to call again in a few days, my heart felt lighter. The family I'd left behind was doing fine, with no sign of Muirloch, and that's what I'd hoped for. I could withstand this separation if it ensured they stayed safe and out of harm's way. I felt buoyant as I walked into the grocery store, referring to the notes on my phone to pick up the items we needed for the next few days.

It was Saturday, so the store was busy. I pushed my slowly filling cart through the aisles, dodging more than one group of neighbors who'd stopped to chat about the concerns every small town had. A century ago, it was the same in Arrington at the new general store, which seemed to be more of a meeting place than a store at times. Back then, our neighbors would discuss new residents in the area, wolves attacking a rancher's livestock, or any number of things important to them. Now it seemed the most important thing was if the local minor hockey team would make the playoffs.

I carted my purchases to the parking lot, still smiling at how little things had changed over the years.

Until I saw the group of men standing next to Chris's truck.

There were four of them, all white and all dressed similarly—jeans and flannel jackets over long-sleeved T-shirts. They seemed to be of similar ages, probably between twenty-five and thirty. A pickup with dual rear wheels was parked a spot or so over, and two of them leaned casually against it on the side closest to Chris's smaller truck. The other two stood between the vehicles, their stances telling me they were ready for a fight. Anger poured off the four of them in varying intensities, but they were all clearly pissed at me for some reason I couldn't fathom.

I paused a few meters from them. "Good day, gentlemen. Can I help you?"

One of the guys standing between the trucks stepped forward. I didn't need my ability to see he vibrated with poorly contained rage. His eyes flashed orange—a clear sign of a shifter on the edge of his control—and a low growl reverberated between us. "Yeah. You can tell us what the hell you're doing in Clearwater."

I arched a brow and indicated my cart full of cloth grocery bags. "Shopping."

"Don't be a smartass," the leader snapped. "You're in *our* territory. Uninvited and unwelcome."

I raised my hands in a gesture of peace. It wasn't clear what sort of shifters these guys were, but I suspected were-wolves—they were the most common, though I hadn't realized there was a pack in this area. "I'm not a shifter, and I'm not looking to make any plays for your territory. I'm vacationing here for a couple of weeks."

"Bullshit." One of the guys leaning against the truck straightened and stepped away from it. "You're definitely not human, though you look like it right now. So you've gotta be a shifter."

The leader bared his teeth. "Cancel your vacation. Go back to wherever you came from."

"I'm not going to do that. I'll be gone in about ten days, and we don't need to cross paths during that time." I started for the other side of Chris's truck, but the leader jumped to intercept me. He shoved at the cart, jolting it out of my hands. Luckily it caught on a stray bit of stone that prevented it from rambling off into another vehicle because I couldn't spare it another thought as a very angry shifter got into my face.

He inhaled deeply, his eyes completely orange now. "What the hell are you?"

I felt the others closing in and wondered how much attention we might be generating. We were at the back of a busy parking lot, out of sight of the main doors of the store, and this section of the lot didn't seem to have many people approaching it. I suspected the cars around us belonged mostly to employees.

"None of your concern," I said. "Let me pack my groceries into my truck, and I'll be out of your way."

"Not good enough."

Behind the leader, I caught the sound of knuckles cracking. Lovely. I was beginning to believe these fools weren't really invested in making me leave their territory—no, they wanted a fight, and this was an excuse to start one. Out of the corner of my eye, I spotted one of the shifters edging to flank me. The emotions of the crew amped up, anticipation and eagerness outweighing the anger, which meant—

I ducked and spun as the shifter who'd attempted to flank me swung a claw-tipped hand. Instead of his fist connecting with my head, mine slammed into his nuts. He went down with a wheeze and a gasp.

The leader was on me next, from behind, his claws scratching against my scalp as he yanked my hair. One of the other remaining shifters flew at me, teeth and claws extended. I cocked my elbow and jerked it back into the leader's nose. Blood sprayed onto the side of my face as he stumbled back, stunned. I shoved the flat of my foot into the other shifter's gut, and he staggered, catching himself on the side of their truck.

As the three of them regrouped, grasping that I wasn't going to be easy prey, I reached behind me to the small slit in the seat of my pants sealed with Velcro. I was wearing one of the pairs of athletic pants I usually wore around the mansion. Josh had taken it upon himself to modify my casual pants with a tail slit, even if I rarely used it. I didn't like acknowledging my tail existed. But it was a good—and unexpected—weapon in a fight. I hadn't had much opportunity to fight since I'd been cursed, but I'd made sure I knew how to use my tail to its utmost effectiveness. A warrior learned all the weapons available to him, or he died in battle.

The leader and one of his cronies still standing charged me while the third shifter dragged his injured friend out of harm's way. I whipped my tail around, the sharp, spade-shaped tip slashing across the leader's knuckles. Not a deep cut, but one that would sting, especially in that location. The leader hissed in surprise, and I followed through with an elbow to the side of the head while he was distracted. He fell to the ground, stunned but still conscious. With a quick shift of my stance, I spun and delivered a reverse hook kick to my other attacker's head. He went down too, groaning.

I caught the eye of the last man standing. His eyes darted from me to his friends on the ground and back to me, clearly trying to decide whether he should try to avenge his defeated brethren or live to fight another day. Not that any of them were in danger of dying—I hadn't hit them that hard.

Indicating the group leader with a nod, I asked him, "This your alpha?"

He shook his head.

"Good. I'm glad for your pack." I really was. This hothead was going to get his people in trouble—I could only imagine the sort of problems he'd find for them if he were in charge. "Tell your alpha I won't be seeking him out, nor will I look for any further trouble. But should I be attacked again, I'll defend myself. Got it?"

"Got it," he growled.

I retrieved my cart, keeping an eye on the shifters as they stayed where they were, on the ground or otherwise. It took only a few minutes to get my bags of groceries into the truck, then I got in, started it, and left the parking lot.

A few kilometers down the road, I pulled into another lot and spent a few minutes breathing. It was one thing to have a fight while I was on duty—it didn't happen often, but it did happen—and another entirely to have one while I was doing something so mundane as grocery shopping. My hands shook, so I wrapped my fingers around the steering wheel, leaned my head against the headrest, and closed my eyes.

Then it hit me.

What if this had been a distraction while Muirloch attacked Chris and Frankie?

Chapter 11

Chris

"Do you think it's too much?" I tilted my head as I looked at the arrangement I'd put together in an enamel camp mug. A few evergreen boughs, a couple of pinecones, and two bare branches I thought were kind of pretty. "Or too little?"

"It's fine. Stop worrying about it." Frankie continued fluffing the worn, lumpy pillows on the couch. Or trying to, anyway. They were so old that there wasn't much fluff left to them.

"I'd rather have flowers for him."

"Good luck with that in February."

"Seriously, though—do you think it's okay?"

Frankie gave up on the pillow he was working on with a huff. "If I'd known you were a worrywart..." His hazel eyes sparkled as he trailed off, and he smirked.

Distracted from my examination of the table's centerpiece, I stalked in Frankie's direction. "Oh yeah, what?"

Predator recognizing predator, Frankie stepped back from the couch to give himself room to move if I struck. "I would've stayed away from you on New Year's Eve."

I prowled closer, and he retreated another step. "No, you wouldn't have."

"Uh-huh. Far away. So far, I would've been in the next county." His eyes were twinkling now as he edged to the end of the couch.

"I would've followed," I promised. "Once I had your scent, I would've followed you anywhere."

"And if—*if*—you caught up to me?"

I straightened from my stalking stance, pretending I'd abandoned the game in favor of thinking through what I would have done in that situation. As I hoped, Frankie relaxed slightly too. His scent surrounded me—the usual crisp mint, heightened with his arousal. It hit me like an aphrodisiac.

"Well, I probably would have..." I hummed like I was thinking. Then I leaped around the couch and grabbed his arm before he had a chance to run, thanks to my reach. "Pounced!"

We tumbled to the floor, laughing, and I was all too happy to pin him there. He struggled, but I could tell it was all for show—there was no strength behind it and he was giggling. I worked my way up his body until we slotted together like we were meant to, his legs opening to cradle my hips as I braced my hands on either side of his head. Our groins rubbed together, and just like that, I was hard as fucking nails.

Frankie's giggles broke off into a groan as he thrust against me. "Gods, that feels so good."

"Yeah."

It felt like it had been forever since I'd been with someone. Normally I found company for the night—or an hour or less—at a gay bar, but I hadn't done that in ages. Ever since moving to Arrington, actually, now that I thought about it. First, it was because I was still considering wooing Teague, and then it was because I'd found Frankie and realized I had two mates and not only one.

"We sh—" Frankie gasped and arched his neck. "We should stop."

"Yeah." We'd decided we'd talk with Teague about everything tonight. Explain the mates thing, hence my attempt at a season-appropriate bouquet. We really should stop...for now, anyway. Maybe we could carry on later, with Teague watching.

That would be so hot.

"You ever bottom?" Frankie asked breathlessly.

"Fuck, yes." A shiver raced through me. "Not often—most guys see my size and want me to top. But I fucking *love* being filled with a cock."

"Dirty talk too? You're gonna kill me." He wrapped his hand around my neck and pulled me down for a hot and heavy kiss.

The rest of the world disappeared. There was only Frankie—my mate—writhing beneath me, every movement telegraphing his want, his need, and heightening my own. His taste exploded over my tastebuds, and time ceased to matter. All I knew was him. The small groans and whimpers he made. The feel of his lips and tongue dancing with mine. The sensation of our hard dicks sliding against each other, layers of material be damned. We should stop, but he was my *mate*, dammit.

Frankie grabbed my ass and pulled me even tighter against him. "Oh my gods, Chris."

"I want you naked," I growled in his ear. "I want my cock sliding into you, hard and fast. I want to mark you, fill you with my scent so everyone knows you're mine."

"Chris."

"And then I want you inside me. Can you imagine that? My legs over your shoulders as you pump into me? Your hair brushing my chest—"

The door opened, slamming against the wall. Instinctively, I scrambled back from Frankie as I called up my beast, ready to attack whoever was threatening my mate.

Except it was my other mate.

"What the fuck?" Teague demanded.

I blinked the sex haze out of my eyes—not an easy thing since Frankie's arousal was so ripe in the air—and took in Teague's appearance. He was in his living stone skin, not his human one, and his tail flicked behind him. His *tail*. I'd seen it before, but only once, and it was easy to forget he had it. It was tipped with a sharp-looking spade-like end and swung side to side as though he were an angry cat. There was a rip in his shirt—no, not a rip. A slice.

"What the fuck happened?" I demanded, getting to my feet.

His purple eyes flicked to my crotch. "I get attacked at the grocery store, and you're here *fucking*?" Around us, things rattled—the stools, the pine boughs in the mug, the oil lamp on the table next to the couch.

"Attacked?" Frankie stood and tried to get near Teague, but Teague held him off with an outstretched arm.

"All the way back here, I'm thinking Muirloch had gotten to you, that the attack was a distraction or a delay tactic, and I walk in and..." He stopped, his chest heaving.

Frankie held out his hands in a calming gesture. "We're okay. Take a few breaths."

Instead of following Frankie's suggestion, Teague's fiery purple eyes fastened on me. He marched past Frankie, nudging him aside to get in my face. "What the fuck do you think you're doing with him? He's half your age, you prick."

My eyes narrowed and I firmed my stance, ready for the fight Teague seemed to want. "So?"

"You're old enough to be his father!"

"And you're old enough to be the great-great-great-grandfather of both of us! What fucking difference does it make?"

"You're taking advantage of him."

"I'm right here," Frankie rumbled.

"I'm not taking—"

"Then I didn't see you pinning him down and humping him?" Teague shoved my shoulder, but I didn't move. The rattling started again, harder this time. Absently, I noted that my centerpiece toppled, the boughs and pinecones scattering across the table.

"Jealous?"

As soon as the word left my mouth, I knew it was the wrong thing to say. The ashy skin of Teague's face flushed pink and he charged me. I stumbled with the onslaught, and we crashed to the floor, shaking the cabin with a whole lot more than Teague's temper. He landed on top of me, his teeth bared, and I realized for the first time that, in this form, he had fangs.

Before he could get more of an advantage, I used my greater bulk to reverse our positions. For the second time in a matter of moments, I found myself on top of my mate, except this one didn't open his legs to welcome me. I straddled his upper thighs instead. He glared as I wrapped my large hands around his wrists like manacles to keep his talons from doing damage he'd regret later.

"Calm the fuck down," I ordered.

"Fuck you!"

This was a version of Teague I'd never seen. Emotional, passionate, fiery. He normally kept himself so locked down, so politely cold, that I'd mistakenly thought he didn't feel things strongly.

How wrong I'd been.

Giving in to my instincts, I captured his mouth with mine. His stone skin was cool against my lips, much cooler than Frankie's, but I enjoyed the contrast. After a second, I realized he wasn't kissing me back, and I remembered —asexual.

I broke off, panting, and drew back to look down at him. "Sorry, I forgot. Is kissing—"

He twisted one hand out of my grip, and I braced for a punch. Instead, he grabbed my neck and pulled me down again, slamming our lips together.

Okay, then. Kissing was a yes.

I fell into it, getting lost as thoroughly as I had with Frankie. Teague's taste and texture were completely different, kind of like licking a stone that had been out in the summer sun all day. Earthy and a bit tangy. Coppery too— oh. I'd cut my tongue on his fangs.

He broke away with a gasp. "Did I hurt you?"

I shook my head.

The flare of his eyes had died down, which I hoped meant he was back in control of himself. The cabin had quieted too. "You shouldn't be kissing me."

"Why not?"

"Because you were just kissing Frankie!" Teague's head thudded against the floor, and he gazed at the ceiling. "Can you get off, please?"

"No."

"Chris." Frankie's hand brushed my shoulder. "Let him up. We should all talk."

I narrowed my eyes at the gargoyle beneath me. "Are you done trying to shake the cabin apart?"

"Yes. I'm sorry. When I lose my temper..."

I scoffed as I pushed myself to stand and held out a hand to help Teague get up. "I didn't realize you had a temper to lose."

That earned me a smack to my upper arm from Frankie. "Don't be an asshole, Chris."

"I think it's his default setting." But Teague grabbed my hand anyway and hauled himself up. When he regained his feet, he was well within my personal bubble, but I didn't mind. In fact, I wanted him closer. In my arms.

He cleared his throat and stepped away, but the vehement movements of his tail gave away his feelings. Now I understood why he kept it hidden even when he was comfortable at home. It revealed that despite his cool and calm demeanor, he was anything but inside.

Frankie gathered the remnants of my bouquet, tucked the boughs and pinecones back into the mug, and restored it to its place of honor on the dining room table. "Chris made this for you," he informed Teague with a smirk.

There was more than a little surprise in Teague's expression when he turned to me. "Really?"

I shrugged, suddenly uncomfortable. "Sure. If it wasn't February, I would've picked flowers for you."

"That's..."

I stiffened, waiting for his judgment.

"Sweet." He offered me a small smile and his lightly glowing eyes softened.

Well then.

Frankie, being Frankie, waved us to sit at the table as though he were king of the manor. We obeyed. I sat beside Teague, turned to face him, and Frankie sat across the table. I looked at Teague and then Frankie, wondering where we should start. Frankie also seemed unsure, his eyes contemplative and his brow furrowed.

It was Teague who spoke first. "So you two...you're a thing?"

"Yes," I said.

"No," Frankie said at the same time. He huffed at me and rolled his eyes. "Sort of yes, sort of no."

Teague's lips twisted. "Well, that's clear as mud."

"Remember the New Year's Eve party you missed?" I asked.

"You mean the one where you ambushed me when I got home?"

"That one." I didn't bother to argue that *ambushed* was a strong word because that was sort of what I'd done. "Frankie and I had caught each other's scents for the first time and, well..."

"Shifters have mates. You know that, right?" At Teague's nod, Frankie continued. "My cat knew Chris was mine. But he'd also already made the same call about *you*."

"I recognized Frankie the same way I'd known you were my mate too."

Teague's purple gaze swung between us. "You're joking."

"I know you think Chris's spell messed up your chances of finding your true love," Frankie said. "But he's connected with me. If the spell was truly limiting, would that have been possible?"

"Maybe it's a shifter thing. Connecting on a different level. Maybe—"

"Maybe you're scared," I countered.

Teague jerked back as if I'd slapped him. "Why would I be scared?" His tail whipped from side to side.

"Why *wouldn't* you be scared?" I toyed with one of the

pinecones in the bouquet, tracing its edges. "I know what it's like to get your hopes up. It makes you vulnerable. Even when it's something you want more than life, that vulnerability can make you shy away. The status quo is always safest. You know what to expect with it."

Frankie reached across the table and grabbed my other hand. "Is that how you felt when you moved to BC?"

"Fuck, yeah." I huffed, glancing at Teague. He was watching my fingers as they poked and prodded the bouquet. Easier than looking at my face, I guessed, which was the same reason I was focused on the pinecone. "I made a bad call in *how* we came out here, but the move was the right one. I don't regret it. The only thing I would change would be being open from the start about who I was and why we needed you as much as you needed us."

He let out a slow breath. "Yeah, I know."

The air rushed out of my lungs. I hadn't realized how much I'd hoped for that acknowledgment until I heard it. To know that Teague understood none of my actions had been malicious in nature... "Thank you," I choked.

Then he did the most surprising thing. He took the hand toying with the bouquet and intertwined our fingers. The touch—so benign and innocent—jolted me to my core. I tightened my grip, afraid I was imagining things, afraid he'd pull away before I was ready to let him. But he made no such effort.

"You're right. I'm scared." He tried to make light of his words with a quick smile, but it didn't last, and the words started pouring from him as though he'd burst the cork on a bottle of bubbly. "I'm so scared about fucking *everything*. Muirloch, yes, and if she'll manage to get to my brothers or anyone else in our family. Your family too." He squeezed my hand. "And then there's my job. I don't know how we'll get past the mucked-up video evidence, and the idea I could be arrested or forced out of my job makes me sick to my stomach. And now this." He huffed a humorless laugh. "Is it strange that this idea scares me the most right now?"

Frankie held out his hand, palm up, and Teague didn't hesitate to close the loop between the three of us. When he did, something sparked, like we'd completed an electrical circuit. From the looks on the others' faces, we all felt it, and none of us shied away.

"Sometimes the good stuff is the most frightening," Frankie said. "Like me bringing the others to your house, Teague. Scariest thing I ever did. But the best, and I had an inkling it would be."

"Scarier than drugging a pride of mountain lions so you could escape?" Teague arched a brow.

"Way scarier. I knew I could talk my way out of that if something went wrong. I wasn't sure I could convince you and your brothers that we meant no harm." Frankie lifted Teague's hand to his lips and pressed a kiss to his knuckles. "Do you have any real objections to Chris and I wooing you?"

"Wooing. Good gods." Teague shook his head—not a negative gesture, but one of disbelief. "I...no."

"Nope." I popped the P sound. "That doesn't work. We need to be honest and open with each other if this is going to be a thing. Open and vulnerable." I waggled my brows at Frankie, showing him I'd learned something from our earlier discussion. "So don't hold back."

Swallowing hard, Teague nodded. "All right. How long will it take you to try to convince me I should have sex?"

I stared at him, speechless, but Frankie had no such problems. He sputtered, "You—you really think we'd do that?"

"Are you forgetting what I walked in on?"

"That was between him and me," I pointed out.

"Right. And eventually, you'll get bored with the idea that I want no part of it, and—"

Using my grip on his hand, I yanked Teague forward so our faces were bare centimeters apart. "Listen," I growled. "If you think our interest in you hinges on whether you'll have sex with us, you don't know Frankie or me at all."

"I—" Teague's purple eyes flared briefly, then dimmed. Let him feel the truth of my indignation. Maybe that would convince him.

"Would I love to have sex with you? Yes, I would. I find you attractive as hell. Would I ever try to *make* you have sex with me?" I snorted derisively. "I'm an asshole, but I'm not that much of an asshole. You've made your preferences clear, and I won't go against them."

"Same." Frankie's lips were pressed together in a thin line, a furrow between his eyebrows. "I'm sort of insulted at the question, Teague."

"I had to ask."

Some of the fire in Frankie's expression went out. "I get it. But let me be clear too. There are levels of attraction. Sexual, mental, aesthetic, physical, and what have you. I'm fully attracted to both of you on every level. That doesn't mean I'm going to force my attraction on you or demand you fulfill it."

"But everything I've read says sex is an important connection between partners—"

"In an allosexual world, driven by sex, sex is viewed as the end-all, be-all. That doesn't make it true."

"Allosexual?" I felt dumb that I didn't know that term, but unlike Frankie, I wasn't a walking encyclopedia of LGBTQ+ knowledge.

"The opposite of asexual."

"Oh." I'd have to remember that term.

Teague looked away, a muscle in his jaw ticking. "You can't—" He broke off, then started again, his voice rough. "You can't start this, tell me you're okay with me being me, and then change your mind. That'll break me."

I squeezed his hand, and that made him meet my eyes again. "That's not going to happen."

"You say that now."

"And I'll say it tomorrow, and the day after, and the day after that, until you believe it."

Frankie shook his head. "Actions speak louder."

"Good point." To prove it, I brought Teague's hand to my cheek, encouraging him to open it, and leaned into his touch. His talons scratched through my beard, far gentler than I thought they could be. Closing my eyes, I let what I felt for him pour out of me. Admiration, fondness, the desire to be near him, touching him. It wasn't love, not yet, but I thought it could be very soon. If we nurtured it and let it grow.

When I opened my eyes, Teague's were glowing gently. From his soft expression, I could tell he'd gotten my message loud and clear.

"So, Teague, you're in?" Frankie prompted.

"I'm in." His words were barely stronger than a breath, but we both heard them.

I would have pumped my fist, but that meant releasing one of my men's hands, and I wasn't about to do that.

Frankie's wide grin matched mine. Finally, after a month in limbo, we were moving forward.

"But I've got some ground rules," Teague continued.

"Go for it," Frankie said.

"If you two want to have sex, have sex."

I nodded. "That's a good rule. I approve."

Frankie chuckled. "All right. I don't think you'll need to convince us to follow that one. Do you want to be involved?"

Teague's open expression shuttered. "You just said—"

"You don't have to be having sex with us to be involved," Frankie interjected. "You can be in bed with us, watching, touching, kissing. Or we can do it behind closed doors."

Pink rose in Teague's ashy cheeks. "Um..."

I put up my hand.

Frankie rolled his eyes. "Yes, Chris?"

"I'd like Teague to be with us. At least at first, and if he doesn't like it, we'll adjust."

Teague met my gaze for a few seconds, then nodded. "All right."

"What's your next rule, Teague?" Frankie prompted.

"We talk to each other. No hiding things, no lying to protect someone's feelings."

"Open and vulnerable," I said with a nod to Frankie.

"Makes total sense to me," he said.

"Anything else?" When Teague shook his head, I looked at Frankie. "You?"

"I think we've covered it, but I reserve the right to add something as we go."

"Awesome." I couldn't help it—my grin widened enough that I felt the stretch in my cheeks. "So...want to go to bed?"

Chapter 12

Frankie

My gaze drifted between Chris's eager expression and the rip in Teague's shirt. "We should probably talk about Teague's attack—"

"He's fine, we're fine. It wasn't part of Muirloch's plot." Chris's brown eyes turned impossibly big and soft, like a puppy begging for a treat. "Please?"

Teague chuckled. "Oh my god, I didn't even know 'horniness' was an emotion I could feel until now. He's right—I'm fine, and we can talk about it after. Put him out of his misery, Frankie."

Again, I rolled my eyes—I seemed to do that a lot around Chris—but I couldn't keep the grin from overtaking my lips. "Fine," I said, huffing a mock-aggrieved breath.

Chris let out a whoop, and before I could react, he'd rounded the small dining table, scooped me off my feet, and slung me over his shoulder. I squealed. "Chris!"

Behind us, Teague was laughing, and it was the *best* sound. Seriously. "Don't throw him on the bed. It might not survive."

"Noted," Chris tossed over his shoulder.

When we reached the bed, he grabbed me like he was going to throw me, and for a second, I thought he would ignore Teague's advice—but instead, he placed me gently on the mattress. I looked up at his imposing form, and my mouth actually watered.

Gods, I wanted him like I'd never wanted anyone else. Except Teague, but he was in a separate-yet-similar category in my heart.

As though my thoughts had summoned him, Teague appeared beside Chris, looking down at me. "He's so pretty," he said with a sigh.

"Isn't he?" Chris's brown eyes were still soft but in a different way than before. Instead of pleading, he was appreciative, and a fire was banked in the depths of his gaze, ready to flare to life. "I love how his hair spills out around him like a halo of fire."

Heat rose in my cheeks, and it was an effort not to look away. "Who knew you were so poetic, Mr. Holt?"

"And his features. So fine and delicate, even though he's anything but." Teague grinned. "It's like he's a superhero in disguise. Pretty and alluring, yet one of the fiercest fighters I've ever met."

Okay, now I did have to look away. I wasn't used to being appraised like this or the words of admiration.

"I think you embarrassed him."

"It was only the truth."

"I know it, and you know it, but I think maybe our Francisco needs some convincing." Chris tugged on one of my pant legs. "Off."

Obligingly, I undid the button and zipper of my jeans and lifted my butt so Chris could strip me. Before long, I had lost every stitch of clothing, and when I chanced another look at Chris, he was practically drooling.

"Fuck yeah." There was a low rumble in his voice, his wolf-bear clearly eager to get in on the action.

"Your turn." The words were barely out of my mouth before Chris started pulling off his clothes quickly enough that he tripped over himself and nearly tumbled onto the end of the bed. I laughed, and the last of my embarrassment faded. "Teague? Are you comfortable getting rid of your shirt? I'd like to touch your skin."

Teague hesitated for a second. "I'm not sure you'll like touching my skin, but..." He pulled his shirt over his head and dropped it on the floor. "Okay."

"Come here." I patted the bed beside me, and Teague climbed on. I rolled onto my side to face him. "This okay?"

He nodded. "Yeah."

This close, I could see details I hadn't noticed before. Like his eyes—from a distance, they looked almost solidly purple, no pupil, no sclera. But now I could see that wasn't the case—his eyes had all the usual elements of a human's eye, but they were overpowered by the glow of magic, even subdued as it was right now.

Chris joined us on the bed behind me, and I gasped as his heat pressed against my back and ass. Without my permission, a purr started up in my chest, and Chris nipped at my shoulder, chuckling.

"Purr machine," he teased.

"It's involuntary."

"It's cute," Teague insisted. "We never have to guess when you're happy."

And I was. For the first time in a very, very long time, I was truly and completely happy. I had my men with me—

finally—and life was looking up. All I had to do was ignore the nastiness of Teague's pending court appearance, which was easy to do when Chris slipped his hard dick between my thighs. The crown rubbed my taint and bumped against my balls, and the sensation was so good. *So* good.

Chris found a rhythm, slow and easy, and continued mouthing the nape of my neck and my shoulders. I kept my eyes on Teague, judging his comfort level with us doing this in bed next to him. He seemed absorbed by the expressions crossing my face, his gaze intent.

"Feels good?" he breathed.

Biting my lip, I nodded. "Kiss me?"

I didn't have to ask twice.

Teague moved in slowly, and his cooler-than-human tongue darted out to taste my lips. I opened them with a moan, and he slipped inside. It was a little weird at first—the texture, the temperature—but the idea that I was kissing Teague, *finally*, overrode everything else. His scent surrounded me, warm stone and the acrid tang of his magic seeping into every pore. I welcomed it, drawing his essence into my lungs as deeply as I could, closing my eyes as the sensations of Teague kissing me and Chris thrusting between my legs threatened to overwhelm me.

It helped that Teague's kiss remained calm, unhurried, as though there was nothing more than this. There was no finish line with him, nothing we were racing toward. Every other deep kiss I'd shared with someone had an end goal— ramping up to getting into bed if we weren't already there. But not so with Teague. It was enough that we were experiencing this together.

The brush of his hand on my cheek was sweet enough to make my breath catch in my throat. So soft, so tentative.

"Are you really here?" he whispered against my mouth.

In answer, I nipped his lower lip, capturing the supple yet strong flesh between my teeth hard enough that he gasped at the sting.

"Why the—"

I smirked. "So you know you're not dreaming."

Before Teague could say anything in rebuttal, Chris bit my shoulder again, much harder this time. I gasped and arched my neck.

"Got your back." Chris held out a fist, and Teague bumped it.

I couldn't help it—I laughed.

"I think you might be doing something wrong." Teague arched a brow at Chris. "Is he supposed to be laughing?"

"No," Chris growled.

"I can't believe you two fist-bumped over—fuck." Whatever I was going to say was chased out of my brain when Chris grabbed my dick and gave it a firm, long stroke. My arousal had taken a backseat to enjoy the slow loveliness of kissing Teague, but now it came rushing to the forefront. It took only a few slides of Chris's hand to bring me to the edge—

And the bastard left me there, abandoning his hold on my dick to grab my hip instead.

I whined and reached for my cock.

"Do me a—" Chris broke off, panting. "A favor?"

It was like the two of them shared a brain suddenly because Teague grabbed my hand, intertwining our fingers and holding our joined fists against his chest. "Got *your* back."

"You're evil," I gasped. I was so fucking hard and wanted to *come*, dammit. Needed to. "Someone needs to get me off. Right fucking now."

"Bossy," Chris murmured.

"He really is," Teague agreed.

"*Guys*," I whined. "Please?"

Teague kissed my nose. "You're so beautiful like this."

"What am I, chopped liver?"

At Chris's protest, Teague leaned over me to kiss him too. Chris's thrusts stopped as he lost himself in Teague's lips, a feeling I already longed for again. I squeezed my thighs and rolled my hips to remind Chris he had a job to do.

"Fuck." The curse burst out of him with a growl. Teague pulled back as Chris resumed his rhythm, harder and faster than before. "Shit, I'm gonna come."

He pulled away from me, and I almost whimpered until I heard the sound of his hand shuttling along his own dick. A moment later, warmth splashed across my ass and lower back, and I moaned at the scent of Chris's come mingling with my own arousal. Teague still held my hand, or it would be wrapped around my dick, bringing me off as fast as possible. As it was, all I could do was whine again.

Especially when Chris dragged his tongue along my skin, lapping up the mess he'd left behind.

"Chris."

"I'm getting there." His voice was low, his words slurred, his tone absolutely smug as fuck.

"Get there *faster*." My arm, held to Teague's chest, blocked my view of my dick, but I could imagine what it looked like—foreskin drawn back, red and angry, a pearly bit of precome at the tip.

Without warning, Chris flipped me onto my back and angled me so my head was perpendicular to Teague. "Kiss him," he instructed Teague.

I was about to protest that he couldn't order us around

like that—but then he swallowed my cock down his throat, and I screamed into Teague's open mouth. Teague chuckled, but I was so caught up in my dick finally getting attention I barely registered it. I couldn't focus on the kiss. I couldn't focus on anything but sinking into the warm, wetness of Chris's mouth, the suction as he drew back, the explosion of feeling.

I tried to warn Chris, but all that emerged was a nonsensical noise muffled by Teague's kiss. A low growl rumbled in Chris's chest as the first spurt of come hit his throat and he eagerly sucked, clearly wanting more.

I gave it to him. Pretty sure my balls emptied themselves, actually.

Sometime later, I floated back to reality, opening my eyes a slit. Chris and Teague were stretched out on either side of me, Chris still looking smug AF while Teague's expression was somewhere between adoration and amazement.

"*That* is what 'fucked-out' looks like," Chris informed him with a wave at my slack features.

I thought about protesting—because, really, he sounded way too pleased with himself—but my brain was barely functioning and my body didn't seem too keen on participating in anything either. I *was* fucked out, and it felt incredible. So all I managed was "Mm-hmm."

Teague kissed my cheek. "You're cute like this."

"He's cute all the time."

Teague tilted his head in acknowledgment. "True. But he's extra cute now."

Chris nuzzled my cheek and yawned. "Can't argue that."

Teague leaned over me to kiss Chris's cheek, then

pushed himself up and out of bed. "You two rest up. I'll get the groceries and start on dinner."

"We were supposed to cook for you," I protested weakly.

"It's fine. I'll cook. You cuddle."

It was hard to argue when sleep insisted, so I gave in.

Chapter 13

Teague

After we ate, Chris and Frankie shifted and ran off into the woods, and honestly, I was okay to see them go.

I needed to think.

My world had changed so drastically in less than a week that my head was spinning. Framed for a crime I didn't do, in hiding and separated from my family, and now...I had two lovers?

How was this my life?

I washed and dried the dishes from dinner, a task that kept my hands occupied and my mind free to examine the circumstances I found myself in. Being in bed with Chris and Frankie had been...good. Intimate. Perhaps slightly overwhelming. Regardless, they'd lived up to their word— never once had they asked me to do something I wasn't comfortable with. They'd respected my boundaries, as they said they would.

But would it last?

The door creaked as it opened, and I turned, surprised that Chris and Frankie were back so soon. But it was only

Chris framed in the doorway. He strode to the couch, where he'd left his clothing, and I quickly averted my gaze. I supposed I could look now if I wanted to, and enjoy the feast for my eyes, but it seemed inappropriate.

"Everything okay?" I asked, keeping my eyes on the remainder of the dishes needing to be washed.

Chris joined me at the sink, retrieved a cloth and picked up a plate to dry. "I felt bad about leaving you here to do the dishes. You cooked."

I shrugged. "It's fine. You both needed to run."

He grunted. "I can't keep up with Frankie."

I smiled at his grumbly tone. "Ah, so the truth comes out. You lost him in the woods, didn't you?"

"Maybe." He shot me a sideways glance. "How are you doing?"

"Me?" My brow furrowed as I handed him a new plate to dry. "I'm fine."

He accepted the plate and dried it, but didn't look away from me. "You sure?"

I opened my mouth to respond in the affirmative, then closed it and gave the question the consideration it deserved. "Honestly, I'm processing."

"If it was too much for you..."

"No. Perhaps." I huffed out an amused breath. "No. Mostly, I'm trying to understand how things have changed so much in so short of a time."

"We can slow down. If you need us to. Shifters kind of skip steps when mates are involved."

"I've noticed," I said drily. "Zero to a hundred in three-point-five seconds."

Chris grinned. "That's an accurate description." He stacked the plate on the other dry one, then reached for a mug. "If we're being honest, I wanted to, uh...check in with you. About you and me."

I paused the scrubbing of the next dish, unsure of how to respond to that.

"I know I have a lot to make up for," Chris continued, retrieving another mug from the drying rack. "I'm not going to pretend that sharing some kisses means that you've forgiven me. I've got to earn it."

"Chris—"

"Wait, please." He put the mug down, then turned to face me, leaning one hip against the counter. "I've apologized, and I'll keep apologizing if that's what you need. But I'm hoping that, maybe...we can start fresh? From here?"

The dish I was washing sank to the bottom of the basin with a soft *thunk*. I grabbed the cloth Chris held to dry my hands enough I wouldn't fling water everywhere, then tentatively cupped his cheeks. I rose up on my toes while pulling him down so our lips could meet, and he gave no resistance.

Our kiss was soft and gentle. He let me lead, yet another indication that he was willing to allow me to set whatever pace worked for me. My doubts from earlier tried to rise again, but I squashed them, focusing on Chris. The supple feel of his lips against mine, the rasp of his beard on my chin, his slightly flowery scent that seemed so at odds with his large body and masculine presence. Unbidden, my tail caressed his arm, his side, and instead of pulling away from the touch, he leaned into it.

I have no idea how long it was before we separated, my head spinning from lack of air. Spinning because of Chris himself. He looked down at me with tenderness, his emotions burbling along like a content brook. "Yes," I murmured.

His head jerked up, and for an instant I was confused until I caught the sound too—an engine, coupled with bare branches scraping against metal. Someone was coming up the drive. I assumed my human skin and quickly tucked my tail into my pants—I'd left it out at Frankie's insistence—and followed Chris to the open front door.

An unfamiliar pickup truck appeared, emerging from the trees onto the cabin's front lawn. It was black, bigger than Chris's, with a crew cab holding four large, unknown men. I thought about calling out for Frankie, but he'd probably already heard the engine, and if he hadn't, he was too far away to help anyway. So I stepped up beside Chris and adopted my best "patient cop" stance, waiting for our unexpected visitors to step out of the truck.

When the driver popped open his door, his bright, closed-mouth smile and friendly wave took me by surprise. He was white and old enough to have graying hair. The corners of his eyes crinkled easily as though he were used to smiling and laughing.

"Good morning!" he called over. "How are you doing today?"

Chris didn't say anything, so I answered, "Fine." I let my tone of voice ask *who the hell are you* and *what are you doing here* rather than wasting breath on the questions. The general emotions I got from the men in the truck were curiosity and a bit of fear, which was interesting. Why would they be here if they were afraid of...me? Or maybe they were afraid of Chris? That didn't make any sense either. I'd never met these guys, as far as I could tell with three of them still in the truck.

From the older one, who'd stepped away from the door —but left it open, an escape route if he needed it—I sensed a tendril of fear, but it was subdued, as though he were used to working through any fear he felt. I could respect that—I did the same daily on patrol. He also exuded friendliness. The smile wasn't for show. Whoever this man was, he was looking to be kind and open.

Unless, of course, he knew about my ability and was doing his best to confuse it. I couldn't always feel deception, but in this case, I didn't think he was trying to fool me.

He remained close to the truck, but where I could see him. His hands were at his sides, in plain view, and his stance wasn't completely relaxed, but close enough that I didn't think he would leap for my throat anytime soon. He wore jeans that had been around the block a few times, paired with an open black parka that had a neon-green safety vest built into it. No toque, no gloves, but then, he'd been in a warm truck until a few moments ago.

"I'm Neil Rademaker. You're Teague O'Reilly, yes?"

I frowned. How did he— then the name clicked. "You're Gale's husband's cousin. The fellow who owns this cabin."

His smile widened further. "That's right."

"Coming to check on your property?"

He waved a hand. "Oh, no, no, nothing like that. It's, well..." His grin turned sheepish. "You ran into a few of my...associates in Clearwater earlier, and I wanted to come out here to apologize."

"Those were your...men?" Chris rumbled, clearly unimpressed with this news.

"You're a shifter?" I gasped. "Holy shit, does Gale know?"

"No, nor does her husband. My shifter line comes from the side of my family I don't share with him."

"Wow." All right. Small, weird world.

Chris took a step forward, the threat in his stance unmistakable. "So why did your guys attack my mate?"

Neil's smile fell away completely. "Because they're young idiots without the brains the goddess gave them." He waved at the truck, and the rear passenger door popped open.

I tensed at the sight of the leader of the gang I'd faced the day before. All the bravado and fight was gone from him, and he looked the part of the chastened teenager—shoulders curved, head bowed, trying to make himself small.

"Isaac," Neil barked.

Isaac's head jolted up, and he met my gaze, albeit reluctantly. "I'm sorry for yesterday, Mr. O'Reilly."

"And?" Neil prompted.

"*Dad*," Isaac whined.

"Keep going," Neil ordered, his voice firm.

Isaac sucked in a breath. "Thank you for not hurting us. I mean, much." His eyes darted to his father, and Neil gave the barest nod. Isaac immediately retreated into the truck.

"Your son, huh," Chris said. His voice was still low and rumbly, but his stance had relaxed a bit.

"In this case, unfortunately," Neil growled. "I wanted you to know that this was not sanctioned by my pack. We're happy to have you here."

"Even if I'm not quite what Gale thought?" I asked.

"Even though." Neil tilted his head. "Isaac said something about a tail?"

Releasing my human skin felt like relaxing a muscle. In an instant, my bulk changed, my chest, shoulders, arms, and legs growing wider and thicker. Luckily, I was wearing my usual around-the-house clothes that could withstand the change in forms. I didn't release my tail from its confines though. That was a step too far.

"What—" Neil's eyes widened. "Gargoyle?"

I nodded.

"Shit. I thought you were a legend."

"No legend."

Neil's wide smile returned. "Then I'm doubly glad to make your acquaintance, Mr. O'Reilly, and thankful I offered up the cabin when Gale asked if a friend of hers who needed to get away could use it. I assume she doesn't know about this side of you, either."

"She doesn't, no, and Teague is fine."

"Likewise, call me Neil." He approached slowly, keeping an eye on Chris, his intention telegraphed by his outstretched hand.

Chris and I stepped down to ground level, but before I could take Neil's hand, he froze, his eyes trained on Chris and crinkled at the edges as he scented him. "He's—"

A mountain lion's scream reverberated through the clearing. I whirled in the direction of the sound to see Frankie charge out of the underbrush, aimed at us.

"No!" I held out my hands in a *stop* gesture. "We're good. They're friends!"

Cat Frankie inserted himself between Neil and Chris and me, snarling. Despite the action being entirely unnecessary, it warmed my heart.

Seeing Frankie wasn't going to let him get any closer, Neil remained where he was, not giving any ground and kept his stance relaxed. He jerked his chin at Chris. "He's not a wolf."

"No, I'm not," Chris agreed.

"He doesn't smell right," Neil pointed out. "I thought that was part of your scent, but it's him."

I crossed my arms, annoyance rising at the criticism. There was no malice in it, but it still rubbed me the wrong way. "Like he said earlier, he's my mate. So is Frankie. Is there a problem?"

Neil's eyes widened, but he quickly shook his head. "No problem, none at all. Simply surprised. And wondering if maybe we can help."

Chris frowned. "Explain."

"When my ancestors first came here centuries ago, they befriended the indigenous community, who taught them how to truly connect with the land and their animal side. We've carried that tradition down through the generations." Neil offered a small smile. "I'm not sure what you're afflicted with, but showing you how to do that can't hurt, right?"

Chris gripped the ruff of fur at Frankie's shoulders and glanced at me. The banked hope in his eyes was heartbreaking because I knew it all too well. Wanting to believe there was a solution, but being terrified you were wrong because you usually were. But maybe this time...

I nodded. Whatever he wanted, I'd support him, and Frankie would too.

"I'd...I'd like to try it," Chris said, trying to keep his voice strong, but I'm sure everyone heard the shakiness. "I'm not sure it will help, but nothing else has, so..."

"If I might ask, what exactly is the problem?"

"My family—my sleuth—was cursed about thirty years ago." The flatness of Chris's tone gave away his emotions, telling me exactly how much it still hurt him mentally, let alone physically. "The curse stole our bears but couldn't remove our nature as shifters. Instead, we shifted into the beast you saw. Not a bear, not a wolf, something unnatural. It also made us unable to have children."

"Goddess," Neil breathed.

"We've been searching for a way to break the curse

since." He looked down at his hands buried in Frankie's fur, and the shame rolling off him was almost more than I could bear.

I stepped closer and enfolded him in my arms, whispering, "It's not your fault. It was your dad's, and you've tried your hardest to fix it."

"I've fucked up so much though."

"But not everything." I pulled back and met his watery gaze. "If this isn't the solution, we'll keep looking until we find it. I'm supposed to lead you home, remember? I will."

That was the prophecy Keelan had shared. Three brothers of stone would lead them home. If you'd asked me two days ago about it, I would have scoffed, but now? None of us knew what it meant, but I was going to find the answer. Right here and right now, I was making that promise to the universe.

"You want to visit our pack lands tomorrow?" Neil asked. "Stay for the day, and we can chat about our traditions. In return..." He smiled again. "I'd love to hear some stories from you, Mr. O'Reilly. Including how you were able to fight off four wolves."

That was an easy payment to make. "It's Teague, remember. And sure, I'd be happy to share. Perhaps offer some pointers too, as long as your son promises not to ambush any other strange shifters. Words first, eh?"

"I keep telling him that. Maybe this will be a lesson he'll finally learn." Neil rolled his eyes, and I could feel his doubt paired with his love for his son.

Ah, family.

We agreed on arrangements for Neil and Isaac to return tomorrow to lead us to their home—since we had no signal and no map—and then watched the black truck turn around and leave. Once it was out of sight, Frankie shifted and faced us.

"What do you think?" Before either of us could reply, he continued, "I think this could be really good."

"Yeah? Gods, I hope so." Chris's voice trembled.

Frankie threw his arms around Chris from the front, and I stepped up and did the same from the rear, so we had ourselves a wolf-bear sandwich.

"Like Teague said, there's no harm in trying this. If it doesn't work..." Frankie's voice trailed off.

I picked up the thread. "If it doesn't work, it doesn't work. We'll keep looking."

We'd find a way to break Chris's curse. We had to.

Chapter 14

Chris

The next morning, I was surprised—and not—to find that the wolves' pack lands resembled my family's ranch. The way the crow flies, it was probably only ten kilometers from the cabin, but by road, it took us about forty-five minutes to get to the large black metal gate with the sign *Rademaker Range* arching over it. Neil's son, Isaac, hopped out of the truck when we reached it and pushed it open, waiting for the two vehicles to pass before wheeling it shut again. I was glad to see there was no lock on it—it was meant to be a deterrent to random visitors, not a means of keeping people in.

Not that I'd truly thought Neil was lying or had ulterior motives. After all, I had a paranormal lie detector on my side, and Teague hadn't indicated that Neil wasn't worthy of our trust.

The laneway was covered in gravel and well-maintained, with only a few inevitable potholes. The freeze-melt cycle in this part of winter played havoc with unpaved roads. The trees had been trimmed back from the lane, not crowding quite as close as they did on the driveway leading to the cabin. We rounded a curve, and my breath caught at the sight before us.

It was probably once a mountain meadow, one they'd expanded to make room for the enormous log house sprawling before us. It had the same general look as the cabin we'd borrowed but more refined, with a red metal roof, a wide staircase leading to the front double doors, and a wraparound veranda. Other houses were scattered past the main one, each larger than our cabin but clearly intended for one family each, whereas the main house could house multiple families.

Frankie, seated between Teague and me, let out a low whistle. "Nice place."

"Right?" I was a little jealous. I mean, I loved the ranch back in Arrington, but this was next level. "Wonder how much land they have."

"Plenty, I'd guess." Teague angled his head to look up through the trees at the mountain looming over the meadow. "I'm not sure I'd like to live full-time in a space so close to a mountain though."

"Why?" Frankie asked.

"Rock slides." Teague shuddered and sat back in his seat. "You ever hear the story of Frank, Alberta?"

Frankie frowned and shook his head. "No."

"I found out about it while researching the history I missed after I woke up. Not sure how I came across it, but half the town was destroyed by a rock slide in the middle of the night in 1903. It gave me nightmares for weeks."

"Awesome. That was a worry I didn't need, Teague. Thanks."

"You're welcome. Happy to share."

Neil parked next to a handful of other vehicles by the main house, and I pulled in beside him. As he emerged from the SUV, a few other people popped out of the house and stood on the veranda, watching us as we got out. The vibe was cautious but welcoming, which I could appreciate.

A woman with blond hair showing a few strands of gray trotted down the steps to greet Neil with a kiss. "Hey, you. These are our new friends?"

"Yep." He turned to us with a smile, an expression he seemed to wear a lot, and beckoned us forward. "Lisa, this is Teague O'Reilly and his mates, Chris and Frankie. Sorry, I didn't get your last names."

I offered a wave. "Chris Holt."

"Frankie Smith."

"Frankie's a cougar and Chris is a bear." Neil tilted his head back and forth. "Sort of. Long story, but he's here to do some learning. Teague, Frankie, and Chris, this is my mate and wife, Lisa Rademaker."

"A pleasure to meet you," Teague said, all old-world charm. Frankie and I murmured something similar.

"Right, then." Neil clapped his hands. "Let's get you all fed, then we can tour the property and start showing you our traditions."

Breakfast—or rather brunch—was a casual affair of thick-cut ham sandwiches on homemade bread, with sweet pickles, also homemade. I was a bit surprised to discover it wasn't Lisa who made the pickles and bread but Neil. Apparently, he was the preserves and baking guy. The fact he didn't adhere to stupid gender roles made me warm up to him even more. Although, I probably should have guessed it by how he hadn't reacted to Teague having two male mates. In fact, no one had when Neil announced it.

Gods, what would it have been like growing up with a man like Neil as a dad instead of the one I'd been saddled with? Ugh. Going down that track would only fuel the resentment that still simmered in my gut. I hated the fact that thirty years later, I still despised the man as strongly as I had when I found out what he'd done and how it had impacted his family. Time was supposed to heal all wounds, but that one had festered and refused to scab over.

After eating, we walked around the main house and the handful of other houses surrounding it. Neil explained that the original lodge had burned to the ground in the early 1980s, and they'd rebuilt it in the same style, only with updated amenities and technology. The other houses were pretty much identical, each with one-and-a-half stories and three bedrooms, all built in the years after the main house went back up.

"We're going to put two more up this summer," Neil said. "Isaac and the three others you met at the store need their own space. They're going to room together for now, but eventually, when they're ready to settle down, we'll put up a couple more for them."

Teague frowned, his lips twisting up. "I'm sorry, but I have to ask. How are you affording all this?"

"Ancestors who found a gold mine and a logging firm my grandfather founded," Neil answered easily. "We do sustainable logging and were one of the first in the province to follow those practices, actually. Gramps made a name for us, and we've kept it going."

"How much land do you own?" Frankie asked.

"A lot." Neil's eyes twinkled.

"Which means...?"

"Twenty thousand acres here and another twenty for the logging to the north."

My mouth dropped open. I'd thought the four thousand acres at the ranch near Arrington was incredible, but to live on have five times that? A dream. "Holy shit. You must have some epic full-moon runs."

"I can't lie. It's amazing. Knowing no one will disturb us or build close to us is...freeing. I've chatted with other pack leaders in the province, and that's a constant worry for those closer to urban centers."

"I bet."

Along with giving us a tour of the property, we met several of Neil's wolves. They all seemed happy, welcoming, with wide smiles and open expressions. I watched Teague's body language every time we met someone, and it remained loose and easy, reassuring me that what we saw was what we got: a content pack who respected and adored their leader.

It made me feel like I'd made the right decision, agreeing to let them try to help me.

As we finished the tour, Neil called out to a few wolves nearby. "Dean, John, Sophie, and Ellen, can you take Mr. Holt to the circle, please?"

"Call me Chris, please. You're not coming?"

"Unfortunately not." Neil looked disappointed at that too. "From past experience, your visit will take a few hours, and I can't be gone that long today. Otherwise, I'd love to go with you."

The folks Neil had called over looked pleasant enough —a white woman, a brown-skinned woman, and two Black men, all around my age—but a spurt of uneasiness went through me at the idea he wouldn't accompany us. He was the only one we knew here, and I wasn't sure I was ready to walk into the woods with three unknown wolves. "What about Teague and Frankie?"

Neil's expression turned regretful. "I'm going to recommend they stay here."

"No," Frankie said immediately.

I was with him—I did *not* like the idea of being separated from my mates for any length of time in foreign territory, no matter how friendly it was.

"Hear me out," Neil urged. "This is a journey he needs to go on alone. If either of you is there, he'll be distracted from it."

"If they're not there, I'll be distracted," I growled.

"No, I get what he's saying," Teague interjected. "If we're there, part of your instincts will be focused on keeping track of us and making sure we're protected. But if we're out of sight—"

"If you say 'out of mind' next, I'm going to be pissed," I warned him. Maybe I wasn't the book-smartest, but if he thought I was dim enough to forget about my mates when they weren't around me, we were going to have a serious talk.

He chuckled and gripped my shoulder. "I wasn't. We'll look out for each other, okay? You're off duty for the next few hours."

I met his unique gaze, the blue of his eyes tinged slightly with purple, and bent to kiss him softly. I wasn't sure I'd ever get used to the experience of kissing Teague, how unhurried it was, how intimate and amazing, but lacking in any building urgency. For him, kissing was the beginning, middle, and end, and it was surprisingly freeing. I didn't have to think of what came next when we kissed—I could simply enjoy the feeling of his warm lips, his tongue shyly dancing with mine, the soft, content sigh that escaped him. After a few seconds—or more, I lost count—I pulled back and brushed my lips against his forehead.

"Hey."

That was all the warning I got before Frankie's hand

slipped around the nape of my neck and pulled me down to him. Where Teague's kiss was like a softly bubbling brook, Frankie's was a raging torrent of a river during the spring runoff. Forceful, a little dangerous, and thrilling to the core. Frankie's kiss told me in no uncertain terms that I was his, *theirs*, and if I knew what was good for me, I'd come back to them in one piece. I was *claimed*, thank you very much. He devoured me, our teeth clashing, our tongues tangling, the minty taste of him nearly overwhelming me. Maybe it wasn't totally appropriate for our audience, but fuck it, I didn't care.

When he drew back, it was with a gasp, his eyes glowing orange with a promise of more when I came out on the other side of whatever this experience would be. Vaguely, I noted a couple of whistles of appreciation from the wolves nearby, but I ignored them in favor of my mates.

"Be safe," Teague said. He slid a hand across Frankie's shoulders and pulled him close.

"I will." As if there was any other option. I didn't know what awaited me in the woods, but nothing would prevent me from returning to my men.

THE "CIRCLE" was...a circle.

I wasn't sure what I'd expected when Neil mentioned it —a roundish clearing, maybe—but no, it was a perfect circle, as though the trees had decided to grow around the space. I couldn't see any sign of lumber being cut to make it, but then, if it were as old as suggested, that evidence would be long gone. It was big enough to seat a dozen people around the perimeter, more if they got cozy, and the interior was carpeted with grass that was strangely green despite the season. I'd gotten used to not seeing snow everywhere this winter—unlike back home, where it first snowed in November or December and stuck around until April, BC saw a lot of melts between snowfalls. But generally, the melts exposed bedraggled brown grass, not this lush greenery.

It was weird.

My expression must have shown my uncertainty as I hesitated on the edge of the circle because Dean grimaced. "I know. It seems unnatural, but it's always like this."

Ellen, the white woman, added, "Doesn't matter the temperature. This spot never changes."

"Why?"

Sophie, the woman with brown skin, shrugged. "Pack legend says, at first, they thought it was a fairy ring."

I grimaced, knowing all too well that the fae were as real as werewolves and twice as dangerous. "Is it?"

"No. It's a place of healing, a conjunction of earth energy. Magical, but nothing otherworldly about it." Ellen gestured for me to accompany her into the circle. "It's safe. I promise."

I wasn't sure what to expect when I crossed the clearing's border. Tingles, maybe? Definitely not the rush of emotion that swamped me. Tears sprang to my eyes and my throat choked up as I fought to keep sobs from spilling out of my chest.

"What the—" I managed, gasping.

"It's okay. It happens to everyone." Ellen's eyes were watery too, and Sophie, Dean, and John seemed similarly affected. "It's cleansing. Let it out."

With a soft cry, I did. I sank to my knees, spearing my fingers through the lush grass to reach the soil beneath, and wept. I'd cried over the past thirty years—not often, but I had. I wasn't as stoic as Teague or as positive as Frankie, and sometimes, the hopelessness of what my family faced overwhelmed me. But those incidents had been nothing like this, a storm of tears that dripped down my cheeks and chin to land on the earth of the circle.

Finally, the storm slowed to a mere trickle. I sat back on my heels and swiped a hand over my cheeks, a bit embarrassed. "Sorry," I said, my voice rougher than usual.

Dean shook his head. He and John were sitting cross-legged on the other side of the circle, their expressions understanding and patient. Ellen and Sophie were next to me, close enough to help if I needed it. "Don't apologize. Like Ellen said, it happens to everyone, especially on their first time here."

Understanding dawned. This was why Neil recommended Teague and Frankie stay behind. If we'd sensed each other's distress during that cleansing bout of emotions, I'm not sure we would have made it through without bolting back to the main lodge. I inhaled deeply and wiped away the last tears. "Okay. I think I'm ready."

"Good," Sophie said with a gentle smile. She and Ellen moved a few feet away from me, and I noticed that with the way Dean and John had already arranged themselves, they were all an equal distance from each other. "Go into the center of the circle, then sit down again."

I followed her instructions, rising shakily to my feet, walking forward a few steps, then sitting cross-legged like everyone else, even though the position was awkward for my long, bulky legs. It felt weird to be singled out like this, but it was meant to help me, so yeah, I had to be the focus. Didn't make it less uncomfortable though.

"Close your eyes," Sophie said. "Concentrate on your breathing. In for four, out for four."

I did as she asked, counting off four seconds for each breath in and out. Slowly, my emotions settled, leaving peace in their wake. I felt light, like I hadn't in, well, ever. I'd always carried the burden of my father's actions on my shoulders, but now, it seemed as though someone had lifted it away, if only for a few moments. Once I left the circle, I knew it would come rushing back. But I wouldn't think of that.

"Seek out your wo—sorry, bear." Sophie's voice was low, even, and easy to listen to. "He's always there, but in this place, you're closer together than you've ever been."

I wasn't sure what that was supposed to mean since how could my beast and I get any closer than sharing a body? But even as that thread of doubt wiggled through my thoughts, I felt him more strongly than ever, and I *got* it. When I was human-shaped, my beast was lesser. When I was beast-shaped, my human side was lesser. In this circle, we were *equal*.

It took my breath away.

Why call me beast? The words in my head weren't words but images, impressions, emotions. I understood their meaning as though he were speaking English. *I bear. You bear.*

I opened my eyes to find my companions had disappeared from the circle, and a big, hulking, beautiful grizzly bear sat in front of me. Though he looked solid, his fur ruffling in the breeze, I knew he was something only I could see. And gods, but the sight brought a lump to my throat. *This* is who I was supposed to be. A piece of my identity I'd lost when I was a teenager before truly getting to understand it. I had lived without since. Seeing my beast in his full, true form *hurt*.

Because despite what he was saying, we weren't *this* anymore. We were something else, twisted and ugly.

"I'm not, not anymore. I haven't been a bear for thirty years." I was vaguely aware I was speaking aloud, but it didn't matter.

We always bear.

"But—"

He growled. *No. We* always *bear.*

I wanted to argue because I'd seen my shifted shape in a mirror, and it was decidedly not a bear, but I felt his resolve and stubbornness on this point. He wouldn't budge, so I let it be. Hell, maybe he was right.

Wait.

Wait, *wait.*

"Are you saying the curse *didn't* take our bears?"

A snort and that eye roll was more human than bear. *Always bear. Might not look like bear, but is. Shift corrupted. But bear? Bear not.*

If that were true—and my bear had no reason to lie, if he even knew what lying was—that meant everything I'd believed for most of my life was wrong. Our bears weren't gone, but blocked by a corrupted shift.

He sat with finality, and I imagined I could hear the *thump* as his rear impacted the ground. *Understand?*

"I...no."

Ugh. He bared his teeth in frustration and balanced on his hind legs so he could wave a paw in a very human-like dismissive gesture. *Human brain stupid.*

I laughed. He sounded so fed up, and all right, I could understand why. "If our bears aren't gone, and it's only our shift that's corrupted, how do we fix it?"

He swiped at his muzzle with an enormous paw. *Uncorrupt it.*

It was my turn to roll my eyes. "Sure. Why didn't I think of that? Should be simple."

He showed his teeth again. *Bear here. Human there. Connection between damaged. Fix connection. Uncorrupt shift.*

"You make it sound easy."

Is.

"It's not, or I would've figured out how to do it already."

He thudded back to his front paws, giving me a look I'd classify as a flat stare if he were human. It was full of doubt.

Maybe I deserved it. After all, I'd had no idea our bears were still bears.

"Do you know where I can start?"

Call me bear.

I frowned. "I don't understand."

No. You don't. Need work on that. He returned to standing with a grunt and started to lumber away from me.

"Wait!"

At my shout, he stopped and looked over his shoulder. He didn't say anything, and I didn't know what to say. The thought of him walking away and never seeing him again— made my throat tighten.

"Don't leave," I begged.

Never leave. Never. Always bear.

Then he disappeared, leaving me alone, confused, and grieving a part of myself I wanted to know better.

Chapter 15

Frankie

Day three after our visit to the wolf pack, and day three of Chris waking up early and disappearing from the cabin. If he hoped Teague and I hadn't noticed him leaving every day, he'd be wrong. We were all squished into one bed, and there was no way to extricate himself without us being aware. The first morning, Teague had wrapped me in his arms and whispered that Chris needed to work through the complex emotions his session in the woods had dredged up, so I'd settled back and let him be. This morning, though, Teague was snoring away—and, honestly, gargoyle snores were way cuter than they had any right to be but were still a deterrent to me falling back asleep—so I slipped out of bed, intent on following Chris outside.

"Frankie."

I froze. "I thought you were asleep."

"This bed shakes anytime someone moves, and so does the cabin." Teague pushed up on one elbow. "What are you doing?"

"Chris left again."

"I know. And?"

I crossed my arms. "It's been three days."

"He needs to work through—"

"I know, you said. But why does he have to do it alone?"

Teague opened his mouth, then closed it. "Good question."

"What if he's going out there alone because he doesn't know he can lean on us for help?"

I'd thought about that a lot over the past few days. Being together was still so new. Emotionally, instinctually, I understood that Teague and Chris were mine, but intellectually? My brain had a hard time adjusting to the idea that *me* was now *we*. The other two had to be having similar difficulties. We'd all been self-contained for so long. Teague had always relied on his brothers, of course, but he was still the oldest, the one they turned to when they needed help. Chris had his entire sleuth looking to him for leadership. And me? I had Nikki, Sarah, Henry, and Chase, and now the O'Reilly family...but none of them truly knew me. I wasn't sure if I wanted them to.

That was something I needed to work through.

"All right," Teague said, pulling on a long-sleeved T-shirt. He already wore a pair of soft athletic pants, and wonder of wonders, his tail was visible, twitching like my cat's did when we were on the hunt. "Let's go."

I let him pass me, then reached out to run a finger along the smooth skin of his extra appendage. He jerked to a stop, and his tail rose as though it was looking for more caresses.

"What are you—"

"Giving every part of you a little love." I smiled.

He stayed frozen for another second, motionless as he processed what I'd said. Motionless except his tail, of course. It seemed to have a mind of its own, reaching out for my hand. I grabbed it above the sharp spaded end and gave it a gentle, playful tug.

Teague shook his head and left the cabin.

The clearing around the cabin was empty, but that wasn't much of an obstacle to tracking Chris down. I could follow his scent easily. We each stopped at the outhouse, then I caught our quarry's trail. It led us into the woods, along a faint track that had been used enough to be a permanent element of the forest.

It didn't take us long to find Chris—maybe five minutes, give or take. He was seated, cross-legged, in a tiny area bare of trees next to a creek. The stream was barely burbling at this time of year, though still moving fast enough to escape freezing. I imagined when the spring runoff came, it would turn into something much more ferocious, but right now, it was an almost meditative element.

I could see why Chris had chosen this spot.

He looked up as we stepped out of the brush and offered a small smile. "Finally decided to hunt me down, huh?"

"Frankie's idea." Teague moved to Chris's far side and sat, mimicking his position. Their knees touched, and neither of them seemed to mind. Though we'd all committed to this, I knew there were *things* Teague had to work through regarding Chris.

Unlike the two of them, I wasn't keen on setting my butt on the cold, damp earth, so I selected Teague's lap instead and stretched my legs out onto Chris's. Neither complained, other than Teague letting out a grunt as he took my full weight.

"Three days is enough brooding time," I said.

"I wasn't brooding."

I arched a brow.

"I wasn't brooding for the full three days," he amended. "Hard to brood when I'm making you scream my name."

I glanced at Teague to check his comfort level. There was a slight blush on his cheeks, which appeared whenever Chris's dirty-talking side came out, but other than that, he seemed fine. He liked watching the handjobs and blowjobs we'd indulged in so far, and especially kissing whichever one of us was on the receiving end. It was trial and error to find what would make our throuple work, and we were all open to experimentation and setting limits that would keep us happy.

"You *were* brooding enough," Teague said, nudging Chris's knee with his own. "Ready to tell us why?"

Chris shrugged, his gaze aimed at the forest floor, and mumbled something even I couldn't pick up.

"What?" Teague prompted.

Chris sighed. "I've been trying to talk to my bear. Okay? And it hasn't been going well."

"I thought you said the curse stole your bears from you."

"That's what I always believed. Except then I go to this fucking magically green circle in the middle of the winter in the woods in fucking *Canada* and have a fucking conversation with him like I haven't in thirty years. I *saw* him too." His eyes glistened. "I forgot what I looked like in that form."

I leaned forward, resting my forehead against his temple and draping an arm over his shoulders. "Oh, Chris."

"He told me the curse had affected our shifts, disconnecting the human side from the bear side, but he was still there. Always bear," he tacked on with a chuckle. "I don't know how to fix it though. I've been trying."

I kissed his cheek and leaned back but kept my hand on his shoulder. Teague had moved closer too—as close as he could get, anyway, with me sitting on his lap and my legs stretched over Chris's. I squeezed his shoulder rhythmically, much like my cat would knead a prime sleeping spot until it was comfy enough. When I realized what I was doing, I paused, but Chris rolled his shoulder in a gentle invitation to keep going. So I did.

It helped me think.

"Maybe...maybe it's like when you all helped us disconnect from the pride," I started, an idea solidifying in my brain.

"But I want to *connect*, not disconnect."

"Same concept, but opposite," Teague said. "I see where you're going, Frankie."

Good. I wasn't crazy then. "It was ultimately up to us to choose to leave the pride, but we couldn't have done it without the positive energy of everyone in that circle helping."

"If you're saying I need more willpower—"

"No, he's saying that maybe your willpower isn't enough and you need outside support."

The metaphorical light bulb clicked on, brightening Chris's brown eyes. "Oh. You think we can break the curse with positive thinking?"

"I don't know. But it's worth a try, right? We'll get everyone together and—" I jerked my head toward the cabin. "Someone's coming up the drive."

Chris and Teague shared a look. "Bit early for visitors," Teague murmured.

Chris tilted his head, and I knew he could hear the vehicle now too. "It's not Neil's truck." He frowned. "It's two SUVs."

We didn't know anyone who would drive up here in two SUVs, which meant the people coming up the drive were strangers. Teague closed his eyes, and a second later, his gray gargoyle hide was replaced by his pink human skin. His features were softer like this, his cheekbones defined but not the hard-cut lines they were as a gargoyle. It was a little odd to see him like this—I'd gotten used to him being in his gargoyle form all the time.

He poked my side. "Get up. I need to tuck my tail in."

I waggled my brows. "Can I help?"

He barked a laugh. "No. If you do, I'll never get it back in my pants."

Grinning, I regained my feet and resisted the temptation to "help" as Teague took care of business. But my grin faded when I heard the SUVs come to a stop and multiple doors open.

"Should I shift and do some recognizance?" My cat was yowling in my head, eager to be let out so we could better protect our mates. The possibilities of who was at our cabin were...well, not quite endless, but numerous. It could be other members of Neil's pack. It could be Muirloch's minions finally tracking us down. It could be someone from Arrington coming out to find us due to some sort of emergency.

Before we could decide whether I should shift, I caught the distinctive sound of a hard fist pounding on a door. "Teague O'Reilly! We have a warrant for your arrest. Come out with your hands up."

Startled, I looked at Chris, whose pale skin had grown even paler. He met my eyes, his wide gaze matching mine.

"What?" Teague, of course, hadn't heard the command. "What is it?"

"It's the cops. They're looking for you. Another warrant." My breath hitched, then picked up speed as fight or flight kicked in. I started pulling off my shirt. "I'll distract them. Chris, you run with Teague to Neil's—"

Teague gripped my shoulder, halting my movement. "No. We're not going to get Neil involved in this. That's not the way to pay him back for his kindness."

"But—"

He smiled, a sad, soft expression. "If there are cops at our door, way out here, they're probably RCMP. Which means there's nowhere in this country I can go to escape."

"So we'll go to the States!" I was breathing like a bellows now, both panic and my cat riding me hard.

"And what will that solve? You want to be separated from our family forever?" His eyes caught Chris's. "Your sleuth?"

"No." The word came out of Chris, low and gravelly like he was chewing rocks. "Not when I might be close to solving the curse."

I slammed my palms into Chris's arm, shoving him sideways. "You're still putting the goddamned cursed over Teague?"

"Frankie—"

"No! They want to take him, and we can't let that happen. Not again." Because if they were here with another trumped-up warrant, they wouldn't let him back out. And if the "evidence" was as convincing as Muirloch's first attempt...

Teague's hands cupped my shoulders, digging hard into the muscle as I resisted. Finally, he managed to turn me around, mostly because I refused to struggle so much that I hurt him. He bent enough to look me directly in the eyes, and the tiny bit of purple in his gaze flared to life.

"I'm not giving up."

"Yes, you are."

"Frankie." Teague let out an exasperated sigh. "If I want

any semblance of my job to remain after this whole ordeal, I need to cooperate."

"You're worried about your *job*?" The last word came out sounding more like a mountain lion screech than a human sound. "I can't believe the two of you. You've both got the wrong fucking priorities!"

I shrugged off Teague's hands, reminding him I was way stronger than he was in his human form, and yanked off my shirt.

"Frankie—" Chris tried to grab for me, but I dodged him.

"Don't fucking touch me," I growled. "You won't take care of this the way it needs to be taken care of, so I will."

"You *cannot* hurt those men, Frankie."

I didn't even pause in shucking off my pants. "They're here to hurt *you*."

"They're not though. They're—"

"Gods, I'm sorry, Frankie."

I barely had time to register the regret in Chris's words before his muscular forearm wrapped around my neck. He might not be as strong as he would be if his bear wasn't disconnected from him, but he was strong enough to keep his hold even when I struggled against him, my claws jutting out of my fingers and raking through his flannel shirt.

The last thing I was aware of was him pressing a kiss to my temple.

As if that made everything better.

Chapter 16

Teague

"Fuck." I stared at Frankie's limp form in Chris's arms. "I—"

"No choice." Chris was close to tears at what he had to do and held Frankie against his chest in a bridal carry. "He was going to hurt the cops to protect you, and they would have shot him. There was no reasoning with him. Am I wrong?"

Swallowing hard, I shook my head. "No, not wrong. His emotions were overpowering."

Chris shifted Frankie's weight. "He's going to be fucking pissed when he wakes up."

"Beyond pissed." *Enraged* was a more apt description. I hoped he would forgive us when he had a chance to calm down.

"Yeah." He heaved out a breath. "Go."

"I'll see you back in Arrington?"

Chris made a scoffing sound. "Of course."

I started down the path to the cabin, then stopped and turned around, stepping up close to Chris. Angling upward on the tips of my toes, I kissed him, and he let out a soft grunt of appreciation. I wanted to take it deeper since I'd grown fond of kissing like that with Chris and Frankie, but the cops' shouts were growing louder and more insistent.

"I'm not there yet," I said, breaking off the kiss, knowing I might not have another chance to say this anytime soon. "But I think I will be. Don't give up on me, okay?"

Chris knew exactly what I was saying. I could see it in the way his eyes softened and how the tense line of his lips relaxed. "Never," he promised.

I pressed a kiss to Frankie's forehead, silently praying that he wouldn't hold a grudge against us for keeping him safe.

Then I bolted down the trail to meet my doom.

It was a long, long twelve hours until they took me out of the cell I'd been thrown into when we arrived in Arrington to a conference room to speak with Gage. The cop who escorted me removed my handcuffs—thank the gods—then left the room. I checked the cameras, but their lights were dead, indicating they weren't functional at the moment.

"You look like shit," Gage greeted me.

I'd done my best to block out the emotions of my other detainees, but that was a losing proposition. Only sociopaths felt nothing when cooling their heels inside a jail —except maybe resentment and annoyance at the inconvenience. Everyone else was plagued with worry, hope, fear, sadness, a cocktail of powerful ups and downs that poked at me constantly. As a result, the past twelve hours felt like twelve days, and I was exhausted.

But Gage was one to talk. His suit was rumpled, his blond hair showing more than one strand out of place, and his skin was dull. At least the brown eyes he shared with his cousin were bright and sharp.

"So do you," I shot back. "Which one of us was behind bars again?"

"Very funny." Instead of smiling at the bit of banter, Gage sighed and pulled a file folder from his briefcase. "Have they told you what the charges are yet?"

I frowned. "I tried to ask the Mounties who brought me in, but they weren't keen on chatting. I assumed the judge had decided to revoke my release—maybe he didn't like the fact I was up near Clearwater."

Gage opened the folder and looked at its contents for a moment. "It's a drug charge."

Immediately, I shook my head. "It's a *what?* No. No, there's no way."

"None? No other secret meetings?"

"No!" I scrubbed my fists into my tired, burning eyes until I saw white speckles dance across my lids. "Who's accusing me?"

"A sex worker named Deanna 'DeeDee' McGee."

"You've got to be fucking kidding me." I braced my forearms on the table.

"You know the name?"

"It's not the kind you forget. Yeah, I know it. I've arrested her a few times, probably three, and talked to her a lot more than that. Giving warnings, seeing if she had information on a case, things of that nature."

"She's saying you traded drugs for information." Gage scribbled on his legal pad, no doubt noting everything I was saying.

"That's *bullshit.* I would never—"

"Any conflicts with her? Anything she could be trying to get back at you for?"

"No! She was always cooperative when I had to arrest her. I kept a stack of Tim Hortons gift cards on me when I was on patrol in case I came across any folks on the street. She always accepted one with gratitude." I shook my head slowly. "I don't get it. I thought we had a respectful relationship, despite me having to arrest her."

"In her complaint, she's stating that she was too afraid to come forward until she heard you'd been arrested, and she realized she should finally tell the truth—that you'd supplied her with heroin."

It was impossible to comprehend this. "I can't believe... What proof do they have?"

"I don't know yet. I don't think it's as strong as the first complaint, because they're not crowing about it. Was anyone around to witness your interactions with her?"

I closed my eyes. "No," I said after a moment. "I didn't call for backup because I knew DeeDee, and when she gave me info, she made sure we were alone. I assumed so folks on the street wouldn't know she was passing on intel, but... could she have been planning this all along?"

"Was that protocol? Not calling backup?"

"Yes. I radioed dispatch with every action I took. There was no need to redirect Gale off her patrol to help me."

"Do you know the dates where you interacted with her?"

"They'd been in my notes." Which I currently didn't have access to.

Gage made another note and underlined it. "I'll request your radio messages for the nights in question."

"I'm not sure how that will help, but yes, please." I leaned forward. "This had to be instigated by Muirloch. Either she didn't like that I was out of town, or she was concerned I was going to walk on her assault charges. So she doubled down."

"Oh, I have no doubt."

"What if she messed with the radio logs?"

Gage wrinkled his nose and leaned back. "Not likely. The video—I mean, she could have bribed the store manager or...I don't know, whatever she did to alter it. But that was far more accessible than official police radio logs. I don't think she'd be able to worm her way to get access to them."

"Okay." Relief coursed through me, and I let my head droop for a second.

"I think the Crown will push to hold you without bond this time," Gage warned me.

I nodded, looking up again. "I get it. Two accusations so close together—they're worried it forms a pattern of a dirty cop."

"Exactly. So you might be in here for a while." He tilted his head. "Is that going to be a problem? Will you be able to...?" His eyes swept me from my head to my chest, his meaning clear.

"It will get harder the longer I'm in here," I admitted. "During the day it's not so bad, but when the sun goes down, it's more difficult. I'll handle it."

"Good." He lowered his voice. "Your friend Gale has been very helpful."

I let out a shaky breath. It soothed my soul that Gale continued to support me. "Good," I said softly. "I'm sure she'll do what she can to get you what you need." Like my notes. Críost, I hope there was something in them that would help clear me. The logs, too.

"No doubt."

"How are Chris and Frankie?"

Gage closed the folder. "Chris is losing his mind. I take it you finally...got close?" He smiled and waggled his brows.

I couldn't stop the blush that heated my cheeks. "Something like that. And Frankie?"

"I haven't seen him."

A pebble of worry settled in my gut, even as I tried not to read too much into Gage's words. Gage was probably preoccupied on the ranch, whereas Frankie would be at the mansion. I assumed so, anyway. I *hoped* so.

"Could you let them both know I'm okay?"

Gage paused in putting the folder back in his briefcase. "*Both* of them?"

My blush deepened, knowing his question wasn't about notifying them. "Yes."

"Well, damn. Go you. And go Chris, and go Frankie too. I'll have to get to know him better."

"I'm sure Chris would appreciate that."

"I'll definitely pass along word that you're doing all right. To your brothers too."

If my blush got any hotter, my cheeks would burst into flame. I hadn't meant to leave Drew and Rian out of the equation. "Thanks."

"Do your best to stay calm and be patient. I promise I'll be doing my utmost to get you out of here as quickly as I can."

"I know you will."

Gage rose and held out his hand, which I grabbed and shook from my seated position. Then he made his way to the conference room door and rapped on it. Instantly, it opened, and Gage slipped out with a soft "Take care" as a cop I didn't know entered to re-handcuff me and take me back to my cell.

I had to let the wheels of justice turn and believe they'd find out the truth.

Any other outcome was unthinkable, especially now that I might have found the solution to my curse.

Nighttime in the jail was decidedly creepy. Most of the lights were off, only a few left on so there would be no hiding in the shadows or people stumbling around in the dark in case of an emergency. It was quiet too—there were other prisoners, but I couldn't hear them, and their emotions were muted with sleep.

I'd been in the jail at night, but on the other side of the door, bringing someone in to be detained for various reasons —drunk in public, DUI, assault, and so on. Normally it was an in-and-out activity for me. Being locked in a cell was a new and completely unwelcome experience.

First off, the walls were too close. The room was definitely small, but at first, it didn't seem too small. That changed as the hours wore on. Now it felt like the walls were getting closer, and the room was shrinking. Logically, I knew that was in my head, so I tried to ignore it.

Second, there was entirely too much time to think. To dwell on everything I'd ever done wrong, from my ill-fated meeting with Muirloch at the gas station back to my life before the curse. Perhaps if we'd tried to speak with Muirloch before attempting to level her death sentence, we could have avoided this fate entirely.

But then, Drew wouldn't have met Josh. Josh likely wouldn't exist because there would have been no one to save his great-great-ad-infinitum grandparents from the sinking ship. Rian wouldn't have met Logan, and who knew what would have ultimately become of the gentle giant of a professor as he staggered under the weight of his grief over losing his mother and twin brother so close to each other.

And I would never have met Chris and Frankie. Would Frankie and the others have remained trapped in that horrendous pride? As for Chris—my brothers and I were supposed to lead him home, according to Keelan. If we weren't here, would he ever find a cure for his family's curse?

"I can hear you thinking from here."

I jerked up at the familiar and hated voice, stunned to see Muirloch standing on this side of my cell door. She looked much the same as the last time I'd seen her—petite, curvy, her fair skin expertly highlighted with makeup, wearing trendy, modern clothes, and her hair a riotous mass of black curls. How had she managed to get inside the jail, let alone my closed and locked cell? I glanced at the camera in the corner of the cell, but its red ON light was not there.

"Don't worry. I've taken care of that. Temporarily." Her soft laughter was like a chorus of minor-key bells, musical but jarring.

"How are you even here?" I demanded, gaining my feet.

"Am I though?" she taunted me and swiped a hand through the cell's wall. Her digits disappeared inside the cinderblock.

An illusion? That was somewhat more comforting than the idea she'd been able to get into the jail without raising an alarm. But disturbing in the fact that it meant she had more abilities than we'd suspected. I refused to let on that this revelation was a concern.

Crossing my arms, I said, "All right then. Why?"

She smirked. "I wanted to see if you were ready to surrender yet." I kept an eye on her as she moved toward me, fighting my instinct to put space between me and the threat she represented. Her movements were casual, as though she projected an image of herself into jails on a daily basis. "This all would have been so much easier if you'd simply given in months ago."

"Bullshit. You'd subjugated the mountain lions well before we knew of your existence. If all you truly wanted was me, you would have come to us first."

She hummed, not denying it but not confirming either. "Perhaps."

"So what are you truly after?"

She gave me a sideways look through her long, thick lashes, and her smirk widened. "You. But there is a definite appeal to carving out a piece of this modern world for myself. People are so...unaware."

I'd wondered more than once over the past few months why it had taken Muirloch five hundred years to track us down and try to force us to pay our parents' debt. When she disappeared after cursing us, had she retreated to wherever the Fomorians, her people, lived? Was it in another realm, like the fae? If that were the case, she might have spent only a short time there while centuries passed on Earth. That would account for the centuries she left us alone, unmolested, as well as her infatuation with the modern world.

But she wasn't wrong about the general population's lack of knowledge concerning the world around them. Growing up, I'd known about beasties like werewolves or the dangerous magic of the fae. Witches were wise and helpful members of the community. All of that awareness had disappeared over time. It had been so odd seeing it vanish firsthand. Every time we awoke, there was less and less knowledge of the mysterious and arcane in the world, exchanged for the surety and security of science.

People failed to realize that science couldn't explain everything as much as they wanted. It left them vulnerable to creatures like Muirloch.

For an instant, I considered giving in to her. Maybe if I did, I could influence her actions. Protect the people of Arrington. But in the next second, the knowledge of what I'd have to give up hit me in the chest—Chris and Frankie. We could build a life together. It wasn't the life I'd envisioned for myself way back when. No, it was far better. Two men who accepted me? Two men who could possibly love me despite my lack of interest in sex? I had despaired of ever finding one person like that, and now I had two willing to work with me to figure out a relationship that would meet all our needs.

Like hell, I'd give that up to satisfy Muirloch's ego.

"Muirloch—and rest assured I'm saying this with as much disrespect as I can muster—fuck you." I narrowed my eyes. "I will never give in. You will never have me. I will beat whatever challenges you throw at me, and when all is said and done, my family will defeat you and send you back to whatever hell you crawled out from."

With every word that fell from my lips, her expression darkened until nothing remained but rage. It satisfied the part of me that wanted to rend her to pieces for killing my parents and torturing my family. I reveled in the dark emotions, not trying to ignore what I was feeling for once.

"You'll regret those words," she spat at me and disappeared.

Maybe I would. But I wouldn't take back a word of it if I could.

Chapter 17

Chris

"Is that her?"

Gage glanced at the woman walking on the sidewalk, headed in the same direction as we were, and shook his head. "No, DeeDee is blond."

"She could have changed her appearance."

A frustrated sigh escaped my cousin. "We can't stop every woman walking down the street and ask her if she's a sex worker named DeeDee."

Sure we could. And I would if we didn't find her soon. Fuck the consequences.

I'd been holding my sanity together by a thread since getting home the day before. Frankie had woken up a few minutes after the cops took Teague, and damn, he had not been happy. I'd hoped he would cool down on the drive back to Arrington, but no. He'd said one sentence to me during the roughly three-hour drive: "Take me to the mansion."

I hadn't heard from him in the hours since.

My skin was starting to crawl with the separation from my mates. Gage had passed on word from Teague that he was doing all right, but it wasn't the same as being in his presence or hearing his voice. I'd called Frankie more than once, but his phone went straight to voicemail. My apologies on the ride home hadn't done anything but make him hiss—and yes, he'd actually hissed at me, his cat more in charge than the man.

The sooner we found this DeeDee and proved her allegations were false, the better. Then Teague would be released from jail, and we could work on making up with Frankie.

That was the only possible outcome I would consider.

"What about her?" I nodded at another woman carrying two large paper shopping bags from a couple of the high-end shops on Main Street. At least she was blond. And DeeDee's friends on the usual working girls' strip had said she might be treating herself to some new fancy clothes. Apparently, she'd come into some cash recently.

I could guess the source.

"This was such a mista—hold on." Gage eyed the photo on his phone, then squinted at the figure on the sidewalk. "Huh. Maybe. Pull over, but let me do the talking, all right?"

"Sure." At least until it was clear Gage wasn't getting anywhere.

He gave me the side-eye as I found a parking spot, and I ignored him. He knew me. Too well. I mean, if he truly didn't want me to say anything, he would have told me to stay in the truck, and he didn't, so...

Gage pasted on a friendly, non-threatening smile. He was a relatively big guy, like me, though ten years younger and with a more refined look. His blond hair was cropped super short on the sides, with the longer top styled perfectly, and he wore a sherpa-lined suede jacket over a lightweight, dark-green sweater paired with dark-wash jeans. Me, I was in my usual jeans-and-flannel getup. But then, I wasn't a lawyer at heart.

"Excuse me, miss?" Gage called out when we'd caught up to the woman we thought was DeeDee. "Are you Deanna McGee?"

Smart of him to not use DeeDee, which was the name she went by on the street. She paused and turned, shifting her bags to one hand. "Do I know you?"

Hot damn, it was her. I'd stared at her features long enough to be familiar with them, and now that I was seeing her up close, there was no doubt.

"I'm Gage Holt." Gage's expression remained open and friendly, but DeeDee's closed down.

"I don't know that name. Sorry."

"No, I know. I was wondering if I could speak to you for a moment?"

She shook her head and took a step backward. "I don't think so."

"It won't take more than a few minutes."

She took another step back, and I knew she was about to run. So I spoke over my cousin. "Why would you accuse Teague O'Reilly of supplying you with drugs when he was never anything but respectful?"

She froze. It reminded me of a rabbit's reaction to sensing a predator nearby, going as still as a statue before bolting. I spoke quickly, hoping to override the flight instinct and nudge her into fight. I had no intention of getting phys- ical with her, but if she wanted to fight, it meant she wasn't running. "He's sitting in jail right now, wondering what he did to deserve your lies."

"I didn't—"

"Don't try to bullshit me. We both know you did.

Teague is probably one of the most honorable cops in this city, and you betrayed all the help he's given you over the years." DeeDee glanced over her shoulder, and I raised my hands, palm out. "Look, I'm not interested in hurting you. I really just want to know why you accused him."

"Fuck," she muttered. Her shoulders slumped, and I knew she wasn't going to run.

"Can we buy you a coffee?" Gage asked, tilting his head toward a small coffee shop across the street.

"Yeah." She heaved in a breath, then nodded. "Yeah, okay."

A few minutes later, we were ensconced at a round booth in the coffee shop. It was a cute and cozy space, intimate without being too tight. Under different circumstances, it would be a great spot for a date. But I suspected I'd think of it as Interrogation Central after this.

DeeDee circled her hands around her latte, the cup so large her fingers didn't touch. "So he's in jail?" she asked softly.

"In the holding cells at headquarters, waiting for his arraignment," Gage confirmed.

"Shit," she breathed. "I didn't...I didn't think anything would come of it, you know? Everyone knows Officer O'Reilly is a good guy. The *best* guy. I thought I'd make the complaint, they'd go, 'yeah, sure, whatever,' and she'd be happy."

"She?" I prompted.

"I think her name was Mary? No. Maura?"

"Moira?"

DeeDee snapped her fingers. "That, yes."

Muirloch. Not that I'd really doubted it. "Okay, tell us the story."

"A friend told me someone was looking for a girl who'd

interacted with Officer O'Reilly. I agreed to talk with her, and she took me out for dinner. A really nice dinner too. Steak, loaded baked potato, wine, the works. Anyway, she told me she wanted to play a prank on him—cause him a bit of trouble, but it wasn't like they'd take it seriously. I believed her."

Uh-huh. "And how much did she offer you?"

DeeDee kept her eyes on her latte. She seemed far younger than she was at that moment. I knew she was in her mid-twenties, but right now, she looked barely legal. With an internal shudder, I realized that was probably something a lot of men were looking for. Gross.

"Five grand," she murmured finally.

"So you sold out a guy who was good to you for five thousand dollars."

"It's a lot of money!"

A lot of money that she wasted—at least partially—on clothes. I managed to keep from rolling my eyes and leaned back when Gage laid his hand on my arm.

"You know it wasn't a prank." Gage's voice was gentle and persuasive, encouraging her to face the truth.

She nodded, swallowing hard. "I know."

"You need to make this right."

DeeDee looked up, her eyes glistening. "I'm going to get into trouble."

"Maybe. But it won't be any worse than the trouble you've been in before." Gage offered her a small smile. "We can drive you to the station. You'll need to tell them everything—what this Moira said to you and why, what you did, how she paid you, everything."

DeeDee sniffled. "Will I have to give back the clothes?"

Would she have to— Only Gage's hand on my arm kept me from reaching out and shaking some sense into the girl.

From the way his fingers dug in, painful even through the flannel, he was livid, but you'd never know it from looking at him. His gentle smile remained intact, though anyone really looking at him would see it didn't reach his eyes.

"Probably not. Let's go, and then you can get on with your life, okay?" He started to rise.

"Can I finish my coffee first?"

Slowly, Gage settled back down. "Sure, DeeDee. Finish your coffee."

I deserved a fuckin' gold star for not reacting. Just saying.

———

A UNIFORMED COP took DeeDee to a conference room while Gage and I waited in the station's foyer. The wheels of justice turned at a snail's pace, but I was hoping Teague would be able to come home today.

"Except there's still the original charge," Gage reminded me. "They rescinded his release on that."

"Fuck." My skin was absolutely crawling with the need to see my mate. It made me twitchy and itchy, and it was a huge act of willpower not to scratch at my arms or chest. The thought that the cops might wonder if I were a junkie needing a fix kept me—mostly—still. "You think they'd let me visit him?"

Before Gage could answer, I'd popped to my feet and walked to the reception desk. Behind me, Gage let out an exasperated sigh, but he didn't call me back. I'd take that as permission to ask.

Not that a lack of permission would stop me unless it would truly jeopardize Teague's case or something.

I politely held back until the officer at the reception

desk hung up the phone, then I pasted on the friendliest smile I could. "Hi."

"Hello. Can I help you?"

"Maybe. I was wondering if it was possible to visit someone you have in custody?"

"No, I'm sorry."

Okay, Holt, turn up the charm. "Really? He's been in here for a couple of days now, and I'd like to see how he's doing. I'm worried about him."

The officer shook his head. "Our facility is for short-term detention only, so I'm sure he'll be released soon."

Yeah, maybe. But not soon enough for my liking. Gage hissed at me from his seat on the bench by the wall, but I ignored him. "Do you think you could check on his status for me, maybe? See if there's anything concerning in it?" As the officer started to open his mouth, I quickly added, "You don't have to tell me what it says, only if he's okay."

"Chris!"

I held up a hand in Gage's direction without looking at him. I wasn't going to get what I wanted here, but finding out if Teague was doing all right was at least something.

"Sure," the officer said finally. "What's the name?"

"Teague O'Reilly."

"Oh." His expression lost some of its helpful openness. "Yeah, he was released earlier this morning."

"He was what?"

Gage caught my arm and gave me a tug, pulling me away from the front desk while murmuring thanks to the all-but-scowling cop. "That's what I was trying to tell you," he said as he guided me to the main doors. "I'd forgotten I put my phone on silent while we were talking with DeeDee. There was a voicemail from Drew saying they'd picked up Teague and all charges have been dropped."

I allowed myself to be ushered outside as I processed this news. It was amazing. But part of me—a giant part—was asking *why*.

Or maybe more importantly, *how*.

"I don't understand."

"I don't either. I don't think any of us do. But there was a second part to his message."

Shit. I could tell by the way Gage was side-eyeing me that I wouldn't like it. "Hit me."

"No one's seen Frankie since last night."

Chapter 18

Frankie

A few hours earlier

Standing at the front gate belonging to one of the elite houses on Wilhelm Drive, I reflected that this might be one of the dumbest things I'd ever done. But also the most necessary.

It had taken some digging, but I'd finally discovered Muirloch was back with Martin Garrison. She'd stayed with him while she was working with the pride—something Becker, the pride leader, had been conflicted about. He wanted Muirloch all for himself, but he couldn't argue that having an in with Arrington's de facto mob boss was beneficial. In the end, the chaos the pride was instigating prompted Garrison to boot Muirloch to the curb.

I wondered how she'd convinced him to take her back. Had it been magic on her part or pure male greed on his? It didn't really matter, but it was something to think about instead of facing what I was about to do.

I pressed the button on the intercom. It took only a second for someone to respond. "Yes?"

"I'm here to see Muirloch."

"Who?"

Oh right. "Moira Lochlan."

"You're not expected."

"No, I'm not, but she'll want to hear what I have to say."

"Your name?"

"Francisco Smith."

The intercom went silent, and I sucked in a slow, deep breath, trying to keep my heart rate from spiking too high. If this didn't work...

The gate clicked and began to open. "Come to the side door," the voice on the intercom said.

Behind the intricate wrought-iron gate was a gorgeously manicured lawn, with evergreen shrubs molded into simple shapes, like cones and spheres. Some, ones I assumed were particularly delicate, were covered in burlap sacks to prevent snow damage. In the spring, I imagined this yard would be a riot of colorful flowers and other plants. The house itself was as impressive as you'd expect a house on Wilhelm Drive to be—refined white brick with a wide light-gray interlocking stone staircase leading up to the massive, double front door, easily a dozen windows on the front façade, some with balconies, and a driveway that curved leisurely around the side of the house. I followed it, assuming it would lead me to the side door I was ordered to appear at.

I was correct.

The door opened as I approached, revealing a Black guy similar in build to Logan—well over six feet tall and built like a tank—but totally missing Logan's gentle giant vibes. This man looked like he'd happily mess me up if I stepped one millimeter out of line.

"That's far enough." He held up a beefy hand, and I obediently stopped a few feet from the door. His voice sounded deeper than it had on the intercom unless I'd been speaking to someone else. Entirely possible—no doubt Garrison had a whole squad of goons at his beck and call. "Do you have any weapons on you?"

My claws, but I wasn't about to tell him that. "No."

He gestured at me to raise my arms, which I did, and he patted me down. After he was satisfied that I was indeed unarmed, he indicated for me to enter the house. This room was clearly originally a mudroom, but it had been turned into something of a security office, with a small desk bearing a large flashlight, two pairs of walkie-talkies, and an open laptop showing black-and-white camera feeds from all over the property. With this much security in place, I assumed this was simply the forward base and there was a more sophisticated setup somewhere inside the house.

A grunt and a nod at a mat beside the door with shoes told me I needed to take off mine, so I did. He made no move to take my sweater or toque, which was fine. It was still chilly enough in the house, at least this part, that the extra warmth was welcome. Then he led me into an actual-to-gods parlor, clearly set up as a place where guests were to wait until the owner of the house appeared. Filled with delicate and expensive-looking antiques, this room screamed money. After getting used to the brothers' homey space, this one felt intimidating...which was the point, I supposed.

It worked—I had no desire to sit. Instead, I stood in front of one of the windows and looked out on the front yard. It was a gray day, typical for this time of year, with heavy clouds on the horizon. Rain was coming soon, or maybe snow, if it got cold enough.

I wondered if I'd be around when it started to fall.

"Well, well, well."

I turned at the unfortunately familiar lilt and saw Muirloch at the entrance into the parlor. Her curly black hair was captured in a braid, with a few random strands escaping to frame her heart-shaped face. She wore a vibrant pink velour lounge set that hugged her curvy form. Her skin was ivory-pale, and she wore lipstick that matched the color of her outfit. If I didn't know better, I'd think she was any other late-twenty-something enjoying a cozy day at home.

"If it isn't one of my wee lost kitties." Her smile revealed brilliantly white teeth, and I didn't kid myself for a second that the expression was meant to welcome me. Oh no, that was one hundred percent the smile of a predator eyeing her hapless prey. "What brings you into my lair, hm?"

I kept an eye on her as she moved casually into the room and chose to sit on a settee with a busy floral pattern in a muted gold that clashed with her outfit. She draped one arm across the back of it and crossed her legs at the knee, completely unbothered by my presence. And why shouldn't she be? It had already been proven that we were of little threat to her.

"I've come to bargain with you."

"Oh, have you? What sort of bargain?"

I inhaled deeply and shored up my resolve. "I offer myself in exchange for Teague's freedom."

"Intriguing." She drew the word out. "And why would you do that?"

"Because I love him. He's my mate."

She leaned forward, her dark eyes glittering. I hadn't noticed before, but her manicured nails were black and nearly as long as Teague's talons. "That is *delicious*. So you're willing to sacrifice yourself for him?"

I swallowed but ignored the churning of my gut. "Yes."

"Even knowing that if he managed to love you back, you might break his curse?" She laughed at my look of surprise, the sound like minor keys on a piano. "Oh yes, I know about their aunt's manipulation of my curse. Their story is a legend back in Eire."

Every instinct in me was rebelling, but I *had* to do this. Even if I was still pissed at Teague and Chris—especially Chris—that didn't mean I didn't love them. Maybe I hadn't said it, but that didn't matter. I did. And this was the way to save them both.

I was expendable. Always had been, always would be. That's what I'd been in every pride I'd ever been in, and the prophecy that drove Chris west focused on Teague, not me. So this was what I could do, how I could contribute. I'd do it gladly if it helped to save the men my soul ached for. Teague would break his curse by loving Chris. It would be enough.

"Yes," I confirmed through gritted teeth.

Muirloch clapped her hands in delight. "Oh, this is absolutely *brilliant*. I couldn't have dreamed a better punishment for Tadgh for defying me."

"No," I growled, more than a little bit of my cat in my voice. "I'll give you whatever it is you want, but I have stipulations."

She settled back into the settee. "All right, boy. Tell me."

I didn't let her demeaning use of "boy" distract me. "First, Teague O'Reilly and everyone associated with him is to be forever left alone by you or any of your cohorts."

Her eyes darkened, becoming impossibly black. "So you'd take my fun from me?"

"What fun is it to chase and chase and never get anywhere?" I met her gaze without flinching. "You know there's no hope. He'll never give in, and then you'll have to wait another hundred years before you can try again. And I can assure you, it won't happen then either. He'll never forget that you killed his parents."

She pursed her lips, some of the ire draining from her expression.

"But here I am," I continued, opening my arms wide, "willingly offering myself to you. I'll be whatever you want, *do* whatever you want, in exchange for Teague's and his family's freedom. I mean everyone in his household, current and future, and anyone associated with him, including Christian Holt and his family. They're all off-limits from this point forward. And you need to drop the charges and destroy the video you doctored."

She narrowed her eyes. "In return, you become my pet."

My throat clogged, but I refused to show it. On some level, I knew that was what I would be signing up for. She'd always enjoyed controlling the pride, and I was offering a small portion of that power back to her. "I'll be your tool," I agreed. "But not against the O'Reillys or anyone associated with them."

"So you said." She examined me closely for a few moments, long enough that I started to think about what I'd do if she said no. Finally, she drew one long fingernail across her palm. Beads of dark-red blood welled in its trail, and I realized those nails *were* talons. She held out her bleeding hand to me. "I accept your terms."

Sucking in a deep breath, I held it as I willed my cat's claws to come out. I mimicked her action, drawing one across my palm, and joined my hands with hers. "It's a bargain then."

As soon as our blood commingled, I felt the oppressive-ness of her magic flood me. I'd felt it before when she'd had control of the pride, but not this strongly. Then, it had been filtered through Becker down to the rest of us. Now, I was the sole focus.

"Oh yes, I've missed this," she purred, as though she were the cat and not me. "Shift."

I instinctively fought the command, but it did no good. Muirloch's magic was undeniable as it forced me to abandon my human skin. In a few painful moments, I was a mountain lion, my clothes nothing more than a memory as my claws tore through them.

"Good kitty," she murmured.

Pain-filled and driven by instinct, my cat snarled at her.

"None of that, now." More pain ricocheted through me, only to fade after a second or two. "You're mine. You now listen to me. You made this bargain without any coercion, so don't be baring those teeth at me, naughty boy."

She was right.

My cat growled, but only in my head this time. She reached for me again, and I submitted to her touch. Reluctantly, but I did submit. This *was* what I had agreed to.

"I think I'll need to get you a collar," she mused, her long nails sharp against the skin beneath my fur. I held still, knowing those nails could end my life if she so wished. "Something with rhinestones. Or perhaps even diamonds."

I closed my eyes and bowed my head.

Whatever she wanted.

Martin Garrison was not who I expected him to be. For one, he was almost as short as I was in my human form. He carried a significant amount of weight around his middle, which made him look like a basketball on stumpy legs. His pale face had a rosy nose and cheeks, maybe indicative of a drinking problem. I didn't scent any recent alcohol on him, though, so if he did like drinking too much, he kept it under control. What light-brown hair he had left was close-cropped against the sides of his head, and the pot lights in the ceiling bounced off the bald skin on the top.

At first glance, he was anything but impressive and definitely looked like more of an uncle-type figure. Until you saw his eyes. Black and beady, they held no emotion, None. The only thing behind them was intelligence and shrewdness and not a lick of feeling for Muirloch, his guards, or me, one way or another.

"Acquired a pet, dear?" He arched a brow from where he sat behind his desk. As Muirloch approached, my rhinestone leash in her hand—she'd sent out one of the guards to hunt down a matching collar and leash set at a local pet store—he snapped the lid of his laptop closed.

He clearly didn't trust Muirloch. Smart man.

"Do you like him?"

Martin shook his head, a half-smile on his lips. "I don't know what your obsession is with dangerous exotic pets, but yes, he's beautiful."

She sidled up to his desk. "You know I love my dangerous things."

Her eyes glittered, and I knew she was talking about more than just me. If I were human, I would have gagged at her terrible flirting. As it was, I let out a rumble, which earned me a yank on the leash.

"Hush now, you."

"He's tame?" Martin asked.

"Eh." Muirloch lifted a shoulder in a careless shrug. "Is anything that was once free ever truly tamed?"

"Excellent point. I trust you'll keep him under control

and with a low profile? The last thing I want is a repeat of the attention you brought to me this past autumn."

Muirloch pouted. "We discussed this."

"We did, but with this new addition to our household, it bears reiterating." Martin leaned back as Muirloch hitched a hip onto the side of his desk. I obediently sat at her side. "I cannot have the police looking at me, Moira. You do understand this, yes?"

"Of course I understand. And I agree. I'm going to make one small outing with this beautiful fellow, and I promise it won't draw any unwelcome attention." She jangled the leash.

"It better not draw *any* attention," Martin corrected. "Zero. Or you'll be out on your ass as you were in the fall."

Muirloch narrowed her eyes. In that instant, I understood that Martin had no idea who or what she was. Maybe he still would have been as threatening if he did, but I thought not. As far as he was concerned, he was putting up with the demands of someone who was arm candy. She must be good at...*things*...if he was this tolerant.

Gah, I didn't want my brain to go there.

It did make me wonder, though, why she hadn't tried to subjugate Martin. Having a quasi-mob boss under her thumb would have been far more powerful than a mountain lion pride. Garrison had connections, money. Becker had had his lions, but otherwise, nothing.

I was sure it would be something to ponder while I lay awake at night.

A tug on my leash brought me back to the room. "Come along then, kitty."

It was more than the pressure on the lead that had me trailing her like a pet dog. Her power washed over me like a tidal wave, forcing my body to conform to her will and sweeping me along like little more than flotsam on a wave. We'd determined months ago that Muirloch was cursed with impotence—the reason why she hadn't killed anyone directly and instead worked through Becker's pride—but at the moment, her power felt anything but ineffective.

Before I knew it, we were in an SUV, being driven somewhere by one of Garrison's guards. It took a few more minutes before I realized exactly where we were going.

Home.

Wait, no. Not home. Not anymore. The O'Reillys' mansion.

Fuck. I hadn't anticipated she'd want to show me off, but of course she would. To rub my nose and theirs in it. To show us all what we'd lost. It was part of her sadistic nature. Godsdammit. I should have made leaving Arlington a condition of the deal. I let out a low rumble, warning her I wasn't happy, but she blithely turned from her seat in the second row and tapped me on the nose.

"Shush. Let me have my fun," she whispered as though I were a co-conspirator. "I won't harm anyone."

Maybe not physically, but mentally? I should have made that a stipulation too. Here I'd thought I'd been so smart, covering all my bases and making sure she'd truly be impotent when it came to the family I'd left behind, but of course, she'd found loopholes.

In trying to fix things, had I made it all worse?

Chapter 19

Teague

I slouched into the armchair in our living room, letting the warmth of home and safety embrace me. I'd honestly thought I'd never see this again—my brothers and their partners surrounding me. Sarah, Nikki, Henry, and Chase were there too, the familiarity of our furnishings, the release of sitting in my living stone skin rather than hanging on to my human skin with the barest grip.

The only thing missing was the comfort of my mates sitting by my side. Gage had texted, letting us know he and Chris were on their way.

But no one knew where Frankie was.

"He didn't leave a note?"

I'd already asked that, but no one shamed me for it. Sarah bit her lip and shook her head, and Henry looked sadder than I'd ever seen him. Even Chase's youthful exuberance was muted, and he leaned against Nikki's shoulder.

"No note, and he didn't say anything to us. I thought maybe he'd gone out to prowl around as his cat, but we try to let each other know when we do that." Nikki absently petted Chase's head. "I didn't think anything of it at first. He was really mad when he got home."

I nodded, but that was a longer story than I was prepared to get into now if Frankie hadn't shared it.

"Sometimes running around on four paws helps to give us some distance from human emotions," Henry said. "But he's been gone longer than he should've been."

"We aren't certain if he went running in his fur," Logan added. "It seems the most likely, but..."

Right. The most likely, but not the only option. The other that stood out was that Frankie was so mad at Chris and me that he decided to abandon the life he'd started to build here. I wanted to say he wouldn't, but how well did I truly know him?

The answer was simple: I didn't. Yes, I knew parts of him, but looking back on our conversations, I realized Frankie had been careful with what he shared. Especially when it came to his time in Becker's pride. He'd told us the basics, but not everything.

And there was something about the way Sarah, Nikki, and Henry were exchanging glances that told me I needed to ask some pointed questions.

Before I could, the front door burst open and Chris stormed inside. He didn't even bother removing his boots before striding across the room and yanking me into his arms. His hug was...well, a bear hug. The inanity of that description made me chuckle, which quickly turned into a sob.

"It's okay," he whispered, his beard rough against my stone skin.

Two small, softly spoken words, and they shattered me. I folded my arms around his back and shoulders and hung on for dear life as a tsunami of emotions threatened to drown me. In moments, the rest of my family—everyone, including the mountain lions—joined our embrace, and I realized I was shoving my flood of sadness and worry and relief at them without meaning to. But no one complained. In fact, underneath all the things I felt was the steady stream of love and support and an extra helping of relief.

"See?" Chris's voice tickled my ear again. "We've got you. You can lean on us."

Perhaps...perhaps I could. Perhaps, occasionally, I could stop being the stoic, unmovable one and let my family prop me up. I melted deeper into Chris's arms and rode out the storm.

I wasn't sure how long it took for my emotions to run themselves dry, but eventually, everyone moved away and Chris led me to the couch, where he encouraged me to sit. He never let go of me completely, and gods, I needed that connection. The past weeks felt like something of a dream and a nightmare, and I needed to know the good parts hadn't been a figment of my imagination.

"What'd they say when they released you?" The question came from Gage. Chris glared at his cousin, but the younger man simply shrugged. "I'm his lawyer. I've got to ask."

"All they said was the charges were dropped."

"No other details?"

I shook my head. "No, nothing."

Chris propped his chin on top of my head as he cuddled me close. "It doesn't make sense, Gage. Why would they release him before we even got there with DeeDee?"

"You what?" I tried to jerk out of Chris's arms, but he held me tight.

"She admitted she lied. Muirloch bribed her with five thousand dollars." There was a disconcerting rumble in

Chris's voice. "We convinced her to come with us to the station to tell the cops the truth, and while she was doing that, we found out you'd been released."

Gage turned to Drew. "Did they say anything to you when they called?"

"It was Teague who called, actually, so no." Drew's blue eyes were stormy. "I've got to say, deartháir, I'm not impressed with the way your siblings in blue have treated you throughout this whole ordeal."

I leaned harder into Chris. Drew wasn't wrong—most of the cops I'd interacted with since I'd been charged had been eager to judge and convict me without a trial.

It wasn't something I could think about right now.

"Have you heard anything from Frankie?" I asked Chris.

"No," he said softly. "I knew he was mad at me—I got an epic silent treatment on our way home. I was trying to give him space."

"Okay, enough with ignoring the elephant in the room." Rian gestured between Chris and me. "You two?"

"Us three," I corrected.

"Wait." Josh frowned, then his eyes widened. "You three...you mean, you, Chris, *and* Frankie?"

Chris squeezed me to his side. "Problem?"

Josh lifted his hands, palms out. "Absolutely none. I'm glad for you."

Drew grunted and leveled a glare at Chris. "Better not pull any more bullshit on him."

Chris ignored him, which was probably best for the moment. Drew would come around, eventually. He didn't forgive and forget easily, but I was sure Josh would work his magic on him.

"So Frankie ran off because he was mad at you two?" Nikki asked. "What happened?"

Briefly, I explained the scenario at the cabin: the appearance of the RCMP, Frankie's willingness to fight them all to help me escape, and what Chris had done to prevent Frankie from following through with his plan.

"Shit, yeah. That would make him mad enough to spit nails," Henry said, scrubbing a hand over his short, tightly curled hair. He shot a glance at Nikki.

I sat up, intent on the two of them. "If you know where he might be..."

"We don't, I promise. But..." Nikki sighed. "There's probably something you should know about Frankie's time in the pride."

"All the prides he's been in, actually," Henry added.

"What?" When they didn't immediately continue, the dread and worry simmering in my gut came to a boil. "For the gods' sakes—"

"Pride leaders called him a 'tool,'" Chase said.

"Rude," Josh said with a snort.

The term didn't mean anything to me either—except as the insult Josh had understood—but Logan's eyes widened. "I've heard of that before. It's a pride member who's trained from a young age to—" He broke off, and a trickle of horror emanated from him. "Be whatever the pride leader needs."

"Which means what?" Chris growled.

"Manipulation, seduction, murder." As each word fell from Henry's lips, my stomach plummeted to my feet. "Prides aren't like packs, where any fighting is done out in the open."

"Holy shit. Are you saying...?" Rian trailed off like he couldn't even bring himself to form words.

"Frankie's killed before." Chris shifted, putting some

space between us so he could look at me. "Teague? Are you okay?"

Worry cascaded off him, and it took me a second to parse that it was directed at me and not Frankie. It puzzled me for a moment, then I clued in. Just as neither of us had known this aspect of Frankie's personality, he didn't know all facets of mine—nor did I know all of his. We still had a lot of learning to do about each other.

I patted his hand. "I'm fine. I wasn't always a cop, remember."

Drew scoffed. "Perhaps we didn't use that word, dearthäir, but you were always a protector of the law."

I tilted my head sideways in acknowledgment. "True. Protector of the law, not morality. I've killed in the past, as my king required of me. I don't see any difference between that and Frankie's role."

"Except now you're a police officer," Chris pointed out. "That comes with different rules."

"Yes, it does. But am I still a cop?" I grimaced. "I'm not sure I'll be welcomed back. Tolerated, yes, but I have a feeling a number of my colleagues have already convicted me." I shook my head. I didn't want to think about that, not yet. "Something to discuss later. Right now, we need to find Frankie."

All the shifters in the room perked up, turning to face the front of the house. "Are we expecting anyone?" Logan asked. "Because there's a vehicle heading up the drive."

I couldn't imagine who would be visiting unless it was someone from Chris's family looking for him or one of my friendly colleagues coming to check on me now that I was released. But anyone we knew would have called or texted first, and a quick round of checks showed none of us had any missed messages.

Chris growled as he stood and started for the foyer. "If they found another fuckin' trumped-up charge to take you in on..."

I followed, reluctant to face whatever waited on the other side of the door. Maybe it would be good news—Frankie coming home—but my gut told me it was anything but. Call me a coward, but I wanted to *breathe* for a time. I wanted to enjoy the freedom I'd been granted after thinking I'd lost it for good. Could we focus on finding Frankie so I could relax with my men and continue getting to know them?

We filtered out the front door in time to see a large black SUV crawling up the gravel laneway. It stopped a good distance from the house, which only added to the weirdness of its presence. I didn't recognize the vehicle, and from the look on everyone else's faces, they didn't either. The sparkling alloy rims, their radiance slightly dimmed by road spray, shouted that this wasn't a cop vehicle. Then I noticed the make and rolled my eyes. As if any law enforcement agency drove Cadillacs.

The back door popped open, and my heart leaped as a familiar tawny form jumped to the ground. Frankie! I went to step forward to greet him, but Chris's arm held me back—and that's when I saw the collar and leash.

And who was at the other end of it.

Muirloch. She was bloody *beaming*.

"I thought you might be looking for this pretty kitty." She stepped away from the SUV, but only a foot or two, and she left the door open for a quick escape should we make a move in her direction. "I wanted to assure you he was in good hands."

"Let. Him. Go." Chris's voice was guttural, more animal

than man. He was doing better than me. I couldn't utter a word.

The emotions rolling off Frankie were intense. Sadness and regret were easy to pick out as his orange eyes took in Chris and me. Hatred too. But above those, determination and stubbornness. Suddenly, I knew.

"Oh my gods," I breathed. It felt like someone had punched me in the gut.

"What?" Chris demanded.

"You're a smart one, Tadgh, aren't you?" Muirloch smirked. "Such a shame you chose to reject me—we could have done marvelous things together. But your Francisco made some excellent arguments when he sought me out." She paused. "Oh, my apologies. He's not 'your' anything, not any longer."

"What is going on?" Chris's eyes were wide as he turned to me. Frustration and annoyance were beginning to build in his emotions. "What does she mean, arguments?"

"Frankie went to her." I swallowed.

"I got that, but—"

"He gave himself to her." I kept my eyes on Frankie, whose head drooped. "Is that right?"

His regret sharpened. It felt different than if he were in human form, but still recognizable. He whined softly and looked away.

Chris tried to speak, but nothing emerged but a raw choking sound. It was the perfect vocalization of what I was feeling as well. After another try, he managed, "No."

"Oh yes." Muirloch's shark-like smile widened, showing off her sharper-than-human teeth. "Very selfless of him. In exchange for becoming my pet, I agreed to his demands to leave you alone, along with your family and everyone associated with you in the present and future. Once he presented his deal, I had to agree it was a good one. As much as I was eager to break you, Tadgh, I've grown weary of waiting. Dear Francisco made an accurate observation that you would never give in. But there he was, willing to take your place, and I no longer had to expend energy on a lost cause. And"—her eyes glittered cruelly—"there is the fact that, now, he is no longer yours. That is an excellent bonus."

Fury like I'd never felt before surged inside of me. This...this creature had stolen so much from me. My parents, my humanity, my future. And now she was going to steal one of the men I lo—could love?

Distantly, I registered that the mansion's windows were rattling with the force of my emotions. The metal of the SUV creaked. Muirloch's curls bounced and her eyes widened.

There was only one thing I could do. I had to kill her.

I charged.

"Francisco."

Before I could reach her, something heavy hit me and knocked me to the ground. I strained for air for a second, looking up at what had hit me and not quite believing it.

Frankie.

His feline face conveyed regret as best it could. He stood on my arms, holding me down, but his claws were retracted, and he wasn't baring his teeth. It was clear he wouldn't hurt me, but nor would he let me up to hurt Muirloch.

"*Why?*" It came out of me on nearly a wail, a helpless plea to understand.

In response, he bent forward and nuzzled his face against my cheek, scent-marking me. He snuffled in my ear, his breath warm across my stone skin, and his rough tongue slipped out to caress my earlobe. Regret and wishfulness poured off him in waves, and I knew this was goodbye.

"No," I whispered. "Frankie..."

"Francisco." Muirloch gave a sharp whistle, and instantly, Frankie's weight lifted off me as he returned to her side.

I hoisted myself onto one elbow and watched Muirloch shepherd Frankie into the SUV. My heart felt like it was breaking, knowing he truly didn't want to be with her. He wanted to be with us, with Chris and me. What had we done to make him think he was expendable? Did this go back to Chris's actions at the cabin? Surely Frankie understood that!

Chris knelt beside me, bending close to put an arm around my shoulders. "Are you okay?"

I kept my eyes on the SUV as it backed away, then turned around. "I'm..." The *fine* wouldn't come. I wasn't fine. I turned into Chris, shoving my face into his chest, and he hugged me close.

"We'll get him back," he rumbled.

"How?"

"I don't know," he admitted with a huff of breath. "But we'll figure it out. We haven't come this far to give up, right?"

"We don't even know where she's hiding."

"Somewhere that's posh enough to have expensive SUVs and provide her with a driver."

Goddamn. Of course. "Martin Garrison."

I regained my feet and turned to the crowd of my family hovering at the front door. Drew and Rian seemed like they were ready to go to war, and everyone else looked as eager to help.

"Did anyone get the license plate?" I felt dumb that I

hadn't thought to memorize it, but in my defense, I was battling the shock of finding out one of my mates had sacrificed himself.

"I did," Chase said and reeled it off.

"Can you get Milo working on that to confirm that what I'm thinking is correct?" I asked Chris. Milo was his super-hacker cousin, and I had no doubt tracking a license plate would be child's play for him.

"Absolutely. Meanwhile, we plan?"

"We plan," I confirmed.

We had a Fomori to kill.

Chapter 20

Chris

"Maybe we should let it stand." Logan raised his hands as Teague immediately turned on him. "I'm not saying forever," he clarified. "But you have to know she had a singular purpose in coming here. She might say she's done with you, Teague, but you know she's not."

I swallowed the rumble in my throat that had started up at Logan's initial suggestion. We were back inside the mansion, and Milo had confirmed that the SUV was registered to Martin Garrison's legit business.

"Logan, I love you, but turn off your logical brain for now." Rian rubbed his love's arm to soften his words. "If Muirloch had me, would you be able to 'let it stand?'"

Logan's eyes flashed orange. "No."

"Then don't suggest it again." Teague turned his back on Logan, so he missed how the much larger man's shoulders slumped at the dismissal. It was clear he was only trying to help, but Rian was right—this was not a great time for logic.

I wasn't the sharpest tree in the forest, and even I knew this was a trap of some sort. A lure to reel us, to reel *Teague* in. If we stormed the castle of the local drug lord, he'd be inclined to protect himself by whatever means necessary. No doubt Muirloch was counting on a hail of bullets to take us out before we could even reach her. Then she wouldn't have to worry about us, and Frankie's deal would be for nothing.

Well, that wasn't going to fucking happen.

"We need to do some recon." Teague leaned over Milo's shoulder, eyes scanning the blueprints the hacker had dug up from city hall. Somehow. I never understood how he did what he did, but damn, I was glad Milo was on my side. "We need to find out how many guards we're talking about, how many weapons, how many entrances to the building, where Muirloch and Frankie might be."

"You don't think she'll put him in a cage or something in the basement?" Milo asked.

"No. She'll want him by her side so she can revel in knowing he's hers."

None of us really knew Muirloch that well—hell, the brothers hadn't even known she existed until a few months before. But Teague's assessment rang true. She was egotistical and overconfident, and she struck me as hedonistic too. She'd want her plaything close.

"I'm gonna rip that collar and leash to shreds with my claws," I growled. Teague reached out without looking and clasped my forearm. It grounded me.

"I'll scout." The offer came from the last person I expected it to—Gage.

I frowned. Gage was great—I loved him, I truly did—but when he wasn't in his lawyer mode, he could be a bit of a wildcard. "I don't—"

He rolled his eyes. "I recognize that expression, Chris. Give me some credit, would you?"

I wanted to, but this was Frankie we were talking about. I held my tongue, though, and waited for him to continue.

He leaned over Milo's shoulder and pointed at the satellite picture we'd pulled up from Google. "Sneaking around this guy's place isn't going to be possible. His property doesn't have any trees close to the house, and there's nothing else to hide behind. So at best, in animal form, we'd get a count of the guards who poke their heads outside. And that's only if a neighbor doesn't report a mountain lion or wolf sighting."

Right. Now would be the perfect time to know a house cat shifter...if they even existed.

"So the only way we're going to get a good idea of defenses is by legitimately getting inside the house. I can do that."

"No." The word leaped past my lips before I consciously formed it. "No way. What if Muirloch sees you and decides to add a wolf-bear to her shifter collection?"

"That's a risk I'm willing to take."

"And what even makes you think Garrison will agree to meet with you?" I folded my arms. "No. It's not a good plan."

Teague's hand squeezed my arm, and once again, his touch worked its magic. "It's dangerous, but let's hear Gage's idea."

I gritted my teeth but grudgingly nodded. Fine, I'd hear him out, but it wasn't going to change my mind.

"It's pretty simple. Garrison has to have doubts about Muirloch, so we'll capitalize on those. He's already thrown her out once because she drew too much attention to him. If I call him up and hint she's starting to act out again, he may be willing to meet with me. Especially if I come at it from a defense lawyer perspective."

"*May* be willing to meet," I echoed with a scoff.

Gage shrugged. "It's worth a shot."

Teague considered the proposal and after a few seconds, shook his head. "If we had more time for you to set up a relationship with him, maybe. But I don't think cold-calling him to ask for a meeting will work, even if you come at it from a professional angle. I have no doubt he's already got a stable of lawyers."

Gage's eyes narrowed. "But—"

"I also don't want to put you in harm's way. Chris has a point—Muirloch will recognize you on sight."

After a few seconds, Gage's expression softened, and he sighed. "Fine."

"Sneaking it is then." Henry grinned. "Chase is good at that."

Chase puffed up a bit. "I am. I'm fast and smaller than the rest of us, and I know what to look for. I've done this before."

The idea of sending Chase in was as appealing as sending Gage—which was to say, not at all. Even if the boy had experience with scouting, which, what the hell? What kind of pride had Becker been running? I shared a look with Teague, and my doubts were reflected in his eyes.

"We'll be there, out of sight," Nikki said, indicating herself and Sarah. "Just in case."

I hoped "just in case" wouldn't be required. But we needed to get this done as a first step in rescuing Frankie, so I reluctantly nodded, and we began planning how Chase would carry out his mission.

It was too conspicuous to meet on Garrison's street, even if we stayed a good distance away from his estate, so instead, our staging ground was a few blocks over in a park that looked rarely used. There were a few tracks in the mostly frozen mud, and though my senses weren't as sharp as they'd been before the curse, I couldn't detect any recent traces of humans or dogs. The park was well-covered by large pine trees that blocked the light from both the moon and the streetlights, making it perfect for our purposes. At midnight on a Friday, I'd expected to see more activity in the posh neighborhood—people coming home from parties, people leaving parties, people leaving for parties—but it was silent as a tomb. Cold as one too.

Probably not the best comparison.

Teague and I sat in my truck in the little three-car parking lot while Logan and Rian were in Logan's SUV next to us, their heads together as they shared either words or kisses. I couldn't quite tell. Chase and his two guardians, Nikki and Sarah, had arrived with them since my truck sat three people at most, and I wanted to keep the spot in the middle of the bench for Frankie.

He *would* be coming home with us tonight.

Even though I expected it, it was still startling to see three large, tawny shapes melt out of the darkness. My lizard brain screamed danger at me, though logic told me this couldn't be anyone but Chase, Nikki, and Sarah. Rian and Logan popped out of their SUV with the trio's clothes, and in a few moments, we were facing humans with news to report.

Chase stamped his feet and blew on his hands. "Five guards, all inside. It's too bloody cold to be patrolling tonight—their words, not mine, though they're not wrong. Jesus."

Sarah rolled her eyes, pulled an extra toque out of her jacket pocket, and shoved it on Chase's head past his ears.

He looked startled for a second but then grinned widely at her. "You're such a good almost-mom."

She smiled and shook her head dismissively.

"Okay, so yeah. Five guards. All armed. Total people in the house—I'm gonna say twelve. There were three upstairs I couldn't get a good sense of, though one of them was Frankie, so I'm gonna assume the one closest to him was Muirloch and the other one is probably what's-his-name—Garrison. Then downstairs, there were four more. Two close to the kitchen, so I'm thinking that's the help, and then two in that same wing who were—ahem—otherwise occupied." He waggled his brows suggestively. "I don't know how they fit in, if they're guests or what."

"You'd think guests would be housed on the second floor. Maybe in another wing, but definitely not near the servants," Logan pointed out.

"You're right," Teague said. "Look at Muirloch's location. The fact that Garrison isn't sharing his room with Muirloch tells me he perhaps doesn't fully trust her, which isn't shocking. So she's a guest, and she's upstairs. The two you heard downstairs, then—I'm going to guess they're part of the staff. Additional guards?"

"I didn't smell any gunmetal on them."

Rian snorted. "I should hope not, with what they were doing."

Teague shot his brother a quick smile. "No, they'd have the guns stored in a safe. Or, well, they *should*. By law. But...criminals, so who knows if they follow gun safety."

Teague wondering if criminals adhered to gun safety rules was seriously the cutest thing. If we were alone...

"Cameras?" Logan prompted.

"Oh, right." Chase looked at the sky, his lips moving slightly as he reviewed his memory. "Front door, side door, two in the back, and one at the door to the detached garage. I think there might be one at the front gate too, but I didn't want to risk getting too close and getting caught on the front cam."

"Six cameras and twelve people," I mused. The cameras didn't worry me—Milo could take care of them from a distance. "Let's say seven definite combatants, all of which will have guns, plus Muirloch and possibly Garrison, but I doubt he'll endanger himself. That's why he's got guards. Two staff members are wildcards, but I don't expect they'll join the fight." I gently nudged Teague with my elbow. "So...what do you think?"

"We do it. Tonight." His expression showed nothing but determination. "Like Chase said, the cold is keeping everyone inside, so we'll be able to get close to the house without getting caught, especially with Milo taking out the cameras."

"Okay." I threw an arm around his shoulders, pulled him close, and pressed a kiss to the top of his head.

He melted against me. "What was that for?"

"Luck."

We had better numbers and a plan to take them by surprise, but I had a feeling we would still need Lady Luck on our side to be successful tonight.

Chapter 21

Frankie

If the past day was any indication, I would not be able to tolerate my time with Muirloch. At all.

She kept me in my feline form, wearing the stupid sparkly collar and matching leash, and controlled me—though her means were more magical than I was used to, I'd been controlled by many pride leaders over the years. I was kind of accustomed to my actions belonging to someone else. That was all terrible enough, but the *petting*. Like I was some overgrown house cat.

I didn't mind contact in this form when it was someone in my new family. Especially Teague and Chris. But she made me sit beside her while she read in the mansion's library so she could pat my head. Or during supper so she could continue to do the same. Even when Garrison commented on how my tail was twitching in agitation—because, yes, there were some ways in which I *was* like an overgrown house cat—she simply laughed it off because she knew I couldn't do anything.

And now. *Now.* She had me lying on one side of her king-sized bed so she could keep petting me while she drifted off to sleep. At least, that's what I thought she was doing, except her eyes weren't closing, and she kept staring at me.

Creepy.

I closed my eyes to escape her gaze. She didn't say anything, but one of those low, discordant chuckles left her lips, so I figured she knew I was faking sleep. Eventually, the petting stopped, and then she rolled over, her touch disappearing from my side.

Fucking *finally*.

Part of me thought I should get up and *do something* now that she was asleep—the human part. The cat part of me was in charge at the moment, though, and we'd been up and tolerating shit for the entire day. We needed sleep.

We had another day of this nonsense to prepare for, after all. I huffed and allowed my cat to pull my human mind into slumber.

I should have known sleep wouldn't bring peace.

It brought nightmares. Ones where Chris and Teague berated me for leaving them, even as I tried to explain why I'd done it. Teague, stoic as always, telling me I was to blame for him going back to sleep in two years. Muirloch cackling away as she skewered my two mates with impossibly long talons. The O'Reilly family and my fellow mountain lions turning their backs on me. Forgetting me.

One instant, I was engulfed in terrible dreams, and the next, I was fully awake, though I didn't open my eyes or move. Something had yanked me back to reality, but what?

It took me a second to realize how quiet the house was. In the middle of a cold winter's night, the central heating should be running, or at least the fan, to keep the warm air circulating. But I heard nothing mechanical. Even the low-level buzz of active electricity was gone.

Clearly a power outage. But was it accidental or intentional? I almost prayed it was intentional. One of Garrison's enemies come to do us all in. It would be better than being petted all day, every day, for the rest of my life. I stayed silent, uncaring if anyone else recognized the potential threat. As far as I was concerned, everyone in this house deserved what they got, including me.

How could I have been so stupid as to think this was a good idea? Sacrificing myself for Teague and Chris—and yes, I'd do it again in a heartbeat. But this was the dumbest way I could've gone about things. Sitting around all day, staring at the object of my hatred, I'd had way too much time to think, and I'd concluded that I needed to work on my reactionary tendencies. If I got the chance.

I'd been hurt by Chris's actions and Teague's obvious support of them. I'd been stymied in my desire to save Teague. So what had I done? Punished Chris by not talking to him and gone off by myself so I could be the great big hero who saved the day. Except I hadn't thought it through. Oh, I'd believed I had, but chalk that up in the Frankie-is-dumber-than-he-thinks-he-is column. I'd somewhat solved the immediate threat—except not really because with Muirloch's visit to the mansion, she showed me that while she might have agreed to my terms, there were loopholes that hadn't even occurred to me. Like her going over there and taunting them with me. She didn't harm them, but if she kept doing that sort of thing—shit, I might as well have given her a knife to cut out Teague's and Chris's hearts.

I hadn't even thought about the fact that I'd actually be weakening the people I thought of as my family. The shock, confusion, worry—I might not have Teague's ability to sense emotions, but my nose and eyes worked fine. I'd hurt more people than Teague and Chris, and I hadn't intended to hurt anyone.

It showed how fucking selfish I was.

Huffing, I closed my eyes again—only to snap them open at a sound that didn't belong. I couldn't say how I knew it didn't belong—after only a few hours in this house, mired in petting, I was shocked I'd cataloged anything outside my misery. I waited for it to come again, and there— a low squeak of a floorboard, drawn out like someone was stepping carefully, watching how much weight they put on the offending piece of wood.

So it *was* an invasion. Cool. A totally involuntary self-satisfied purr escaped me.

Muirloch jolted upright, her dark eyes glittering in the low light coming in through the bedroom window. She glared at me for a second, her head tilted as though she were a shifter too, and then a slow smile spread across her lips.

"Brilliant," she whispered.

She dropped to the side of the bed, out of sight, as the door to her room burst open. I couldn't help but hiss at the sudden intrusion—until I realized who it was.

Teague.

His purple eyes glowed with a fierceness I'd rarely seen from him, and his fangs were bared as he took in the room. His pale gray skin made him look like an avenging wraith, and the gun in one hand and the sword in the other did nothing to dissuade that impression. His tail whipped from side to side behind him, its movements as ferocious as the rest of him.

I did the only thing I could. I jumped off the bed toward him, meowing.

The hard lines of his face softened for a second, probably as a result of hearing a huge mountain lion meow, of all things. But I was *so happy* to see him.

"Stop."

I didn't turn around, but I didn't have to. I felt the power of Muirloch's order like she'd grabbed the ruff of my neck and jerked me to a halt. Straining against the command, I tried to reach Teague. If I could only get close enough to touch him...

Teague's expression hardened, and he raised his gun. "Let him go."

She scoffed. I was frozen in place, but I could imagine what she looked like. Standing on the other side of the bed, her black curls bouncing around her shoulders, wearing the pink T-shirt nightie with a glittery logo she'd gone to bed in. Not an intimidating image, but then, her looks were never what had been scary about her.

"You're going to shoot me?" There was laughter in her voice. "Do you truly think that will kill me?"

"No, but it'll hurt like hell." Without any further warning, Teague fired.

Muirloch screamed, and her hold on me snapped.

"Run!" Teague shouted.

He didn't have to tell me twice.

I sprinted out of the bedroom, my back legs skidding on the hardwood floors until they caught the carpeted runner that stretched down the hallway. Another shot went off in the bedroom, then Teague's heavy feet pounded behind me. My ears were still ringing from being so close to the first shot, but I could still pick up the sound of fighting elsewhere in the house and the unmistakable screams of mountain lions and growls of Chris's wolf-bears.

"Go!" Teague gave me a shove on my rear as my steps

faltered near the top of the stairs. "We're getting you out of here, and then we'll figure out everything else."

Okay. Yes. I could live with this plan.

I careened down the stairs, sliding and leaping more than running. I hesitated for a second at the bottom, forgetting which way to go, but another tap on my hindquarters got me moving again. Then the open door was in front of me. Cold air blew in through it, bringing with it the scents of incoming rain, frozen river water, and hardened muck.

Freedom.

A figure suddenly darkened the door. For an instant, I thought it was Chris, and my heart leaped. But then the man raised a rifle, and I realized who it was—Martin Garrison. I screamed at him, bunching my muscles to do my best parkour off one of the walls to avoid a bullet when someone grabbed him from behind and spun him around.

The gun went off.

The scent of blood bloomed in the air. A scent I knew almost better than my own.

Chris.

I leaped onto Garrison's back, my claws sinking through his clothes to pierce his skin, and snapped my fangs through the nape of his neck, neatly severing his spine. He was dead in milliseconds. I abandoned the corpse without a second thought, consumed by the fact that Chris was *bleeding*.

He was lying on his back, beyond the door, staring at the night sky, his chest a mess of blood. More blood flecked his lips and his skin was pale, too pale. I got down on my stomach and crawled up close, and he offered me a smile that didn't last.

"'S okay," he slurred. "'S okay, doesn't hurt."

No. Please, gods.

"Chris!" Teague skidded to his knees, his sword and gun

falling to the ground. His hands hovered over Chris's wound as though he didn't know where to touch. How to help. He swallowed hard, and I witnessed the cop training take over. "You'll be fine. It's fine."

"Liar." Chris's voice was barely there, and his eyes closed. "I get it now."

"What?" Teague glanced over his shoulder. "Drew!"

"'Bring me home,'" Chris whispered.

I snarled at the same time that Teague snapped, "Don't you talk like that. You're going to be *fine*."

Chris opened his eyes partway and lifted a shaky hand toward Teague. Teague grabbed it, not caring about the blood that coated it. "I wish we could've gotten there."

"Where?"

"Love." His eyes closed again. "We would've. I know it."

His heart was slowing. So was his breathing. I edged closer, wanting nothing more than to touch him with my human hands, cup his cheeks, brush my lips against his. *Don't go*, I wanted to wail, but all that came out was a feline cry.

For all that he wished he and Teague had been able to find love in the time they'd had together, he and I already had. But it didn't matter. When had the universe ever cared about the feelings of the people that inhabited it? I could cry and scream all I wanted, and it wouldn't change the fact that Chris Holt was lying on the cold ground, dying, and there was nothing I could do to stop it. I nudged his side, and Teague brought his hand down so Chris's fingers could feel my soft fur.

Chris sighed. "Love..."

I waited for the second word.

It never came.

Chapter 22

Teague

I was numb.

Other people's emotions hovered at the edges of my consciousness, a jumble I didn't want to unravel, but my own were gone. Or locked away. I wasn't sure which, and I didn't care.

Chris was dying.

If he weren't cursed, his shifter healing might have had a chance to kick in, but chest wounds were bad. Really bad. I didn't know if even a shifter could recover from something like this. Robotically, I sliced his shirt open with a talon, then peeled my own off, folded it, and pressed it to Chris's wound. It was like my brain and body were operating on two different frequencies—my brain knew putting pressure on the wound wouldn't help at this point, but my body, my heart, didn't want to give in.

Could Drew's or Rian's magic help? I had no idea if Rian knew of a rune that might help slow the bleeding or maybe enhance Chris's healing. Drew had once threatened to use his ability to manipulate metal to pull all the iron from someone's blood—could that apply to putting blood back into a person?

I sucked in a lungful of air tinged with copper and screamed, "Aindréas! Rian!"

"I'm afraid they're otherwise occupied, mo stoirín." Muirloch ambled out of the house, feet bare, dressed only in the nightie she was wearing when I'd burst into the room. The bitter breeze made the material ripple around her knees, but the cold didn't affect her. The nightie was splashed with red on the shoulder where I'd shot her, but she gave no indication the wound still existed. I hadn't thought it would stop her for long, but I'd hoped it would have put her down for a little longer. She smiled, showing too-sharp teeth. "Martin's guards are a wee bit tougher than I gave them credit for."

I rose to face her. Behind me, Frankie growled, low and menacing, and moved to keep pressure on Chris's chest.

Muirloch's eyes drifted to Frankie. "Silence."

His growl cut off instantly, a reminder she still held him in her control.

"Better." She tossed her head, flipping her dark curls over her shoulder. "Ah, Tadgh. If only you'd given in, you'd have saved both your lovers."

"Shut up."

Her laugh was as discordant as ever. Unnatural. "Instead, you fought me. And for what? You've lost it all, haven't you? Your lovers, and when you go to sleep and reawaken, your brothers. All that will remain will be me." Her smile widened. "I have waited five hundred years to find you, Tadgh. What's another hundred?"

"You'll never have me. Not in a hundred years or five hundred or a thousand." The rage simmering inside me for centuries frothed into a boil, rupturing the numbness I'd welcomed. I bared my teeth. "Never. Do you hear me? You murdered my parents, stole my life and my brothers' lives, and punished us for a crime that wasn't ours."

"Your parents—"

"Are dead!" My tail flicked hard as I screamed out the words. "You exacted your price! We owe you nothing. Nothing!"

Her dark eyes glittered. "You owe me everything. You *exist* because of me."

Footsteps suddenly crunched on the frozen grass to my right from the direction of the river. "And yet, you never had a deal with Teague or his brothers."

Both Muirloch and I turned at the new voice. My eyes widened at seeing Keelan looking very much not like Keelan. There were...flowers in their hair? And antlers. Because why not.

Nothing made sense.

Muirloch's expression slipped from shock to a deeper rage in an instant. "This is none of your concern, Tuath Dé."

This time, my mouth dropped open. Keelan was a member of the Tuatha Dé Danann?

Keelan's gaze fell to Chris's too-still, bloodied form and Frankie still desperately trying to keep pressure on the wound—the only thing he could do. For a second, Keelan looked as human as I remembered, and regret, fondness, affection, and other emotions rolled off them. They looked back at Muirloch. "On the contrary, this is very much my concern."

The corner of Muirloch's lips lifted in a derisive snarl. "Aw, did your pet get injured?"

Keelan didn't rise to her bait. Instead, they stepped closer until the three of us formed an equidistant triangle.

Only then did they stop. "I'm here to mediate your reparations to the Ó Raghailligh clan."

"My reparations?" She barked out a laugh. "I'm the wronged party."

"Perhaps originally," Keelan stated with a shrug. "But once you killed their parents for reneging on your deal, the matter was concluded. Everything you've done since—"

"They were going to murder me!"

Keelan tilted their head. "You were careless enough to get caught for killing their parents. What did you expect?"

Muirloch pressed her full lips into a thin line. "I am not yours to judge, Tuath Dé."

The smallest of smiles graced Keelan's mouth for a brief second. "My king—and yours—say otherwise." There was something in their voice, some thread of power, that made me think Keelan spoke nothing but the truth. The kings of the otherworld were in agreement on this matter...which, at a guess, didn't bode well for Muirloch.

From the sudden pallor of her skin, she understood that as well. Her shoulders deflated and the power that always emanated from her dimmed.

Then she launched herself in my direction.

I spun, whipping my tail around. The sharp, spaded end connected with something. There was resistance, then...none.

I turned in time to watch Muirloch's head bounce to the ground. Her body followed, landing with a hard thump that reverberated through the frozen ground into the soles of my feet.

Before I could even process what had happened—what I'd done—pain resounded through my body, from the tip of my head to the ends of my toes. I curled forward, catching myself on one hand.

A very human, very cold hand.

I blinked at the pale, pinkish skin, my brain refusing to comprehend what I saw. I hadn't consciously changed form, but I was human. The breeze, which I'd barely noticed a moment ago, felt like knives stabbing the bare skin of my back and chest. I went to flex my tail, only to realize nothing was there.

Nothing.

Well, except for a hole in my pants letting in cold air.

I scrambled to close the Velcro that usually kept it shut, then swung around, falling on my ass, as I finally spotted my tail. It was on the ground, motionless, completely stone, and disintegrated into nothing before I could comprehend what I'd seen. Then Frankie's collar jingled to the ground, distracting me.

He was human again, naked, pressing down on the shirt I'd sacrificed to stop the bleeding. I couldn't tell if it had helped or not. Overwhelmed, I stayed where I was, my fingers losing more and more feeling with every second they remained on the icy ground, but I couldn't move.

Was this real? Had I just killed Muirloch? Had I broken—

No. I couldn't voice that yet, even in my head.

"Chris, come on. Open your eyes. *Please.*" Frankie's voice was rough from disuse, the consonants and vowels more guttural than usual. He glanced up, frantically looking around for help.

I still couldn't move. There was nothing we could do, but I'd be damned if I'd break Frankie's heart even further by saying it.

"*Christian.*" Keelan sank to the other side of Chris's form. They looked upset but not shocked, and I realized Chris was right.

This *was* the prophecy.

I'd thought that what Chris had learned at the Rademaker's ranch was the key, a path to reconnecting with his bear. A path to home. But no—*home* had always meant *death.*

Suddenly I could move again. I pushed to my feet and charged over to the tableau, leaping over Chris to shove Keelan to the ground. "You fucker. You knew this would happen!"

Keelan looked up at me, as calm as ever, despite being supine on the ground. The antlers they'd sported moments ago were gone, as were most of the flowers. They looked almost human once more, but not quite. "It was what he needed to have happen."

"He needed to die?" Frankie snapped. "Are you fucking crazy?"

"Yes, he did." Keelan's gaze didn't waver. "The curse is strongest in him, and he's the gateway for it to affect the rest of his family. For it to break, he needs to die."

Keelan might as well have punched me in the solar plexus. I couldn't draw in a breath. The worst of it was, I knew that if Chris was awake to hear this, he'd tell us to let him go. If it saved his family...

"No. *No.*" The denial ended in a mountain lion's scream. I cast a look over my shoulder to see Frankie had collapsed over Chris's body, his shoulders heaving.

"He needs to die," Keelan repeated, and fuck, if I never heard those words again, it would be too soon. "But then... perhaps I can save him."

Chapter 23

Chris

I sat beside my bear, leaning against his front leg and shoulder. On the one hand, it was weird—I was never meant to be outside of my bear like this—but on the other, it was comforting to know I had a forever companion with me here.

Wherever *here* was.

His fur was surprisingly soft, where the gentle pulses of the breeze pushed it against my face. He smelled like a bear, all musky and earthy, but there was a sweet overtone of wildflowers that made me think his being locked away couldn't have been all that bad. I turned my face to burrow deeper into his pelt, reveling in the connection vibrating between us.

I'd missed it so much.

He grunted and flopped to his stomach, and I found myself draped across his shoulders. Also a good position, no complaints from me.

Should go. Like in the wolves' mystic circle, my bear communicated to me with thoughts and images, but my brain translated them as words.

"Why?" I liked where we were, even if I didn't recognize it. It was quiet, peaceful. It smelled good. It was a good place.

Not place to stay. He grunted and shifted onto his side.

I flipped over so my back leaned against him instead and stared into the pine boughs draped high above us. The sky was blue, the bluest I'd ever seen. There wasn't a cloud in view, and even though I couldn't see the sun, I could feel its warmth radiating down on us, warming the soil we lay on. A few more minutes here wouldn't hurt, right? At least until Frankie and Teague got here.

Wait.

I frowned at the sky, realizing that beyond the wind whispering in the trees and the breaths from my bear, I could hear nothing. No bird calls, no animals rustling in the underbrush. I levered myself to a sitting position and looked my bear in his big brown eyes.

"Where is here?"

He sent me a barrage of images I struggled to interpret. A paw stepping off a creek bank, hovering above the water. A snout crossing the threshold into a dark cave. Twilight descending. Dawn breaking.

I shook my head. "I don't—"

He sat up, grumbling. *Human brain—*

"Stupid, I know. Help me understand." Because as the moments ticked by, I was realizing that if I didn't recognize where we were, how would Frankie and Teague know where to find me?

This time, he sent me images of snow melting, leaves changing, high river waters receding, a footprint in snow disappearing as the snow did. Temporary?

Temporary. Suddenly all the other images made sense—they were in-between moments.

I stared at my bear, and he met my stunned gaze with sadness in his expressive eyes.

"We're—" I choked and my voice disappeared. "Dead?"

I remembered then—the sound of the gunshot, the searing heat of the bullet, then the numbness that expanded outward as Frankie and Teague hovered over me, their lips moving. I clutched a hand to my chest, but of course, there was no sign I'd been injured. This was the afterlife—or a stepping stone to it, at least.

He nosed my cheek. *Should go.*

He didn't mean back to Frankie and Teague. "I'm not ready."

He said nothing but leaned forward in invitation. I wrapped my arms around his neck and buried my nose in his fur.

I WASN'T sure how much time had passed as we sat there. If time even mattered anymore. I guess it didn't, did it? If I was...if I was truly dead, then I was outside the mortal world and its obsession with time. Somehow, that thought was not at all comforting. When I leaned back from my bear, there was no change to our surroundings to give me any hint—the sky was still the bluest of blues, the breeze rustled consistently, and no other creatures had intruded on us. Bear was right. This place was temporary. An in-between. We couldn't stay here.

Even if I wasn't ready for the next stop on our journey.

I swallowed hard. "You'll be with me, right?"

Always. He grunted. *Always bear.*

The familiar refrain brought a small, short-lived smile to my lips. It was a comfort that I wouldn't be alone. "I—"

Breaking off, I whipped my head around. I swore there was something... "Did you hear that?"

A negative grunt.

Had we stayed too long in this place? Were my senses playing tricks on me? I opened my mouth to say that, when I heard the sound again. Faint, unidentifiable, but there. In a place as unchanging as this, it shouldn't be there at all.

My bear tilted his head, then snorted. *Dunno. Should go.*

He was right. Maybe this was a sign we'd overstayed our welcome. I stood, brushing off my pants automatically, only to discover there was no dirt or other debris clinging to them. So weird.

"Do you know where to go?" I placed a hand on his broad head, my fingers spearing into the fur between his ears.

He grunted and took a step.

"Christian Aaron Holt."

I froze at my full name, little more than a whisper but undeniable. Turning, I peered through the trees to see who was calling me.

My bear took another step.

"Christian Aaron Holt!"

I tugged on my bear's fur to bring him to a halt. "Wait."

Can't trust. His huge head swung around so he could stare at me. *Can't stay.*

"No, I get it, but..." I didn't have the words to explain how I needed to listen to the voice calling my name. I could almost place it.

"CHRISTIAN AARON HOLT!"

Closer now. Louder. But still not quite recognizable. Why couldn't I identify the speaker?

Then—

"Please come home." I sucked in a breath. Frankie.

"We need you." Teague.

Yes. Home. That was where I needed to go. Not into the unknown. I needed to go back to my mates. I couldn't leave them yet.

But how? If Bear was right, this was an in-between place, and there was only one direction I was supposed to go.

"There you are." I recognized that voice finally too—Keelan. "Hang on."

I blinked—

And opened my eyes to a dark sky. Snow fell onto my face, and I sucked in a giant breath as though I'd been underwater and had just resurfaced. My back came off the ground, but Keelan pushed me down by my shoulders. It was too much effort to resist, so I didn't.

Instantly, Frankie leaned over me, his gorgeous, delicate face pale but filled with cautious hope. "Chris?"

I wasn't sure I could form any words—everything felt so off—so I nodded.

Then Teague was there too—human Teague, bare-chested and...shit. I tried to wave a hand at his face, but all I could do was wiggle a finger. "Blue," I managed.

"Huh?" Frankie changed his focus from me to Teague, and his eyes widened. "Shit, Teague, your lips are blue."

Teague gave a wavery smile, and when he spoke, his words were slightly slurred. "It's a little cold, but I'm okay."

Questions swam in my head. Why was Teague in his human skin? Why was the cold affecting him so keenly? None of it made sense, but I was too tired to focus on any of my thoughts. Except, of course, that I was home. My *true* home.

Frankie scrambled to his feet and rushed Teague. "You

are not okay. Oh fuck, you're not even shivering. That's not good." He wrapped Teague in his arms, skin on skin. "Godsdammit, where is everyone else? We need a jacket or something!"

I wanted to keep my eyes open—hell, I wanted to get up and find some clothes to help Teague warm up. But my body felt like it was filled with cement, and my eyelids bore ten-pound weights. A firm, familiar hand pressed on my shoulder. "Rest," Keelan said. "I'll make sure your mates are taken care of."

Trusting my friend, I closed my eyes, and consciousness slipped away.

WHEN I AWOKE AGAIN, I found myself in a king-sized bed with Teague between me and Frankie. I had vague memories of being guided into an SUV at Garrison's, driven back to the mansion, then led upstairs to a room that smelled a bit stale but still like Teague, and collapsing on the bed, tugging Teague's chilled body against my bare chest. I'd had fleeting thoughts that skin-on-skin contact was the best solution for hypothermia, and then I'd fallen off again.

Teague's color was much better, a lovely pink instead of the blue tinge that had taken over. His cheeks were even rosy, and...wait.

Why was he still in his human form? It was an effort for him to maintain his human skin, so he should have reverted to his stone skin while he slept. And for that matter, he shouldn't even have had an issue with the cold.

What the fuck did I miss?

Frankie stretched languidly, like his cat would, and let out a low purr as he snuggled closer to Teague. Eyes still closed, he nuzzled Teague's neck, pressing tiny nibbles, licks, and kisses to the skin. Teague grunted, angling his head to give Frankie more access, though whether he was awake or it was a reflexive thing, I had no idea. At the moment, I didn't care.

What mattered was that we were all here. Together. Alive.

Holy shit, we were *alive*.

Unable to stop myself, I grabbed my two mates and hugged them close. The movement earned a startled *urk!* from Frankie, but he didn't protest. I tucked my nose into Teague's neck, where Frankie had been kissing moments before, and struggled to keep my emotions under control.

"It's okay," Teague whispered. "Let it out."

I released my hold on my emotions, sure I was about to bawl my eyes out and not caring—my mates understood. I knew they did. Instead, though, I laughed. And laughed more, harder, until I was shaking with the force of my guffaws.

We'd beaten an ancient creature. Though I was fuzzy on the details, I knew we had to have or else how would we even be here? We'd beaten death because I knew that's where I'd been when I sat with my bear. After everything, we were fuckin' *alive*.

How amazing was that?

Frankie squirmed one of his arms out of my grip, and his fingers dove into my hair. "I love you both," he said softly, a smile in his voice.

I lifted my head enough to meet his eyes. "Love you too."

Teague swallowed. "I—"

"You're not there yet," Frankie rushed to interrupt.

"And that's okay. We've got time now. The curses are broken—"

"Broken?" I echoed. Well, that explained—

Wait, *curses?* Plural?

Frankie smiled, a wide, joyous expression. "Can't you feel it?"

Too scared to hope, I closed my eyes and focused inside. Instantly, my bear was there, rumbling happily at being in bed with his—our—mates. The urge to keep my eyes closed and drift back to sleep was strong, but I recognized it now. Back when I was a teenager, back when I'd last felt my bear like this, I'd wanted to sleep through every winter. Freaking hibernation.

I laughed, opening my eyes. "I'm a bear again."

Always bear, my bear grumbled.

"So is the rest of your family," Teague said, his very human face creased in a smile as wide as Frankie's.

My breath caught. Saving my family had been my goal since I was a teenager—for two-thirds of my life. To have finally achieved it...I almost couldn't swallow around the lump in my throat. There would be kids now, cubs to teach and play with. A new generation to carry on our traditions and learn from our mistakes.

I couldn't fuckin' wait.

"And Teague...how...?" My brow creased. Clearly, he hadn't broken the curse the way his brothers had, by finding his true love.

"I killed her. Muirloch."

"Sliced her head clean off," Frankie added. "With his tail."

I grunted. "Good." Cupping his face with one of my big hands, I nudged his eyes in my direction. "Are you okay?"

His smile changed in intensity but didn't die away. "I am. It was a long time coming."

"Five hundred years," Frankie said.

"Five hundred years," Teague echoed.

My ordeal hadn't been quite as long-lived as Teague's, but I felt the relief in his voice down to my bones. It was going to take some time for the reality of it to sink in for both of us.

"I'm really glad I never asked you to do anything sexy with your tail now," I said into the quiet that had settled into the room.

Frankie smacked my arm. "Chris!"

"What? Just saying!"

Teague sank into the bed, laughing so hard tears rolled down his cheeks. Then, suddenly, the tears weren't from laughter at all. "It's over. It's finally over."

Frankie cuddled close and kissed his jaw. I wiped away the wetness on Teague's cheeks with my thumb and leaned in close, not caring about his morning breath or mine. "It's over," I whispered, holding his gaze.

Biting his lower lip, he nodded.

"But this"—I touched the tip of my nose to his, then kissed Frankie softly—"this is only the beginning."

He drew in a deep breath and let it out slowly. "Kiss me?"

As if he had to ask.

I braced myself on my forearm and leaned over him, resting some of my weight on his chest and hip. Not all of it though—Teague being one-hundred-percent human was too new for me to make assumptions about what he could handle. I'd have to learn him all over again, like he'd have to relearn himself, but that was okay. We had the rest of our lives.

As with every other kiss I'd shared with Teague, it was soft, unrushed, and rather than focusing on how it ramped up my body for the next event, I concentrated instead on the suppleness of his lips, the feel of his tongue tangling with mine, his mild, well-rested taste, the barely there hint of warm stone in his scent which was already fading into memory.

Biology was biology though. It took me a few minutes to realize I was rubbing my hard, underwear-covered dick against Teague's hip. I broke away with a groan and shifted my butt backward so I wasn't tempted to keep humping him. Brushing hair from his forehead, I kissed the tip of his nose and said, "Sorry. I didn't mean to make you uncomfortable."

His smile was full of understanding, and his eyes...gods, they were so full of emotion, one I wouldn't put a name to until he was ready. "It's okay. Why don't I switch places with Frankie?"

"I've got a better idea." Frankie's eyes, in contrast to Teague's, sparked with lust and mischief. "You ready to take me, big guy?"

"Oh, *fuck* yes." My grin split my face. "How do you want me?"

Frankie slipped out of bed and shucked his underwear, revealing his long, slender dick already standing at attention and waiting for my ass. Perfect. "You two move more into the middle. Chris, stay on your side, just like that." He scrambled to my side of the bed, then froze. "Aw, fuck. No lube."

"There's some in the bedside table. Top drawer." At Teague's words, I arched a brow, and his cheeks flushed. "An orgasm helps me sleep."

"Oh, we are totally going to explore that, don't you

think otherwise." Frankie grinned, and I was in complete agreement. The thought of Teague rubbing one out made me groan, and I really hoped he'd let us watch someday.

Frankie dug into the drawer and pulled out a bottle with a triumphant noise. "Got it. Chris, is your underwear off?"

Oh shit. I knew I was forgetting something. I shimmied out of my boxers and dropped them to the floor. "Now they are."

Frankie tossed the lube on the pillow, narrowly avoiding my head, and bounced onto the bed behind me, wasting no time in getting under the covers and pressing his lithe body against mine. He felt scorching hot, especially the hard rod nudging my backside.

Rather than dwell on the sound of Frankie opening the bottle of lube and the squelching sounds it made—because simply thinking about what would happen next was enough to make me blow—I checked in with Teague. "This okay?"

He nodded. "It's fun, watching you have fun."

"Oh, this is fun, all right," Frankie assured him. Then slippery fingers dove between my cheeks, making me gasp.

"A little warning?" I croaked as he rubbed a fingertip around my rim.

He cackled evilly. "Where's the fun in that?"

Teague's smile widened. "You're in trouble."

"The best kind of trouble," I agreed, my eyes falling partially closed. "Fuck yeah, give me a finger."

"Hold up your leg," Frankie ordered, his voice low and growly.

I did so, holding myself open for him. He took full advantage, sliding first one finger, then another inside of me, working me open. It had been ages since I'd done this with anyone—since I'd even played with myself like this. Stroking one off in the shower was more my usual.

"Feel good?" Teague asked quietly.

I opened my eyes, forgetting when I'd closed them all the way. "So fuckin' good."

He scooted closer. "Rest your leg on me."

"You sure?"

"I'm sure."

My knee draped perfectly over his hip. It was a bit lower than I'd been holding it, but that was all right. Skin-on-skin contact with Teague, while Frankie was touching me so intimately...it was exactly what I needed.

"Fuck. I hope that's enough stretching for you because I can't wait any longer." Frankie's voice was even lower than before, almost more growls than words.

"Do it."

The first push of his cock against my rim burned in the best way. I relaxed into it, welcoming the intrusion, thankful Frankie wasn't any thicker. One of his hands slipped under the space between my armpit and the mattress to hold on to my shoulder, while the other gripped the thigh resting on Teague's hip, his nails sharpening into claws just enough to bite into my skin. Slowly, so slowly, he slid all the way inside.

"Yeah, give it to me," I moaned. "I want all of it."

"Fuck, you're tight." Frankie leaned his forehead against the nape of my neck.

"And you're perfect. Splitting me open." I clenched my ass muscles around his hard length, eliciting a harsh groan. "Move."

Frankie eased back, far more gently than I wanted or needed. I was about to tell him that I wasn't delicate, when he thrust home hard.

"Fuck! Yes. Gods, yes. Pound me. Do it. Fuckin' do it!"

The words pouring out of my mouth became more and more nonsensical with every slam—until suddenly my mouth was occupied with Teague's lips and tongue, swallowing every sound I made. I tried to kiss him back, but Frankie was relentlessly hitting my prostate on every thrust, stealing my ability to think, breathe, or move.

"Oh my gods," Frankie breathed, his rhythm stuttering. "Chris. Oh my fucking gods." He bottomed out inside of me, freezing there, cock pulsing with his release.

I groaned, closing my eyes, utterly satisfied that my mate had found his pleasure with me. My bear rumbled in complete contentment.

And then Teague whispered two magical words. "May I?"

My eyes snapped open to find Teague looking at me with an intensity I'd never seen from him. It wasn't heat in his eyes, not like I'd witnessed with Frankie, but it was definitely need. Wordlessly, I nodded.

His touch was tentative at first as his hand wrapped around my dick. His grip was slick, a surprise that had me groaning in appreciation, and I automatically rolled my hips so my cock slid easily in and out of the slippery tunnel he'd made.

"Good?" he asked.

"Fuck, yes. Just like that." I thrust into his hand then withdrew, my ass still wrapped around Frankie's length. He hadn't softened yet, and good gods, but it felt amazing. "Close. So fuckin' close."

"Yeah, baby. Fuck yourself on my dick," Frankie whispered.

With those words, my animal nature broke free. I bared my teeth and worked my hips, almost overwhelmed with the feeling of Teague's rough palm catching on the bell of my cockhead, and Frankie's length deep inside of me. It took only a couple of more thrusts before I was there, shooting my load onto Teague's hand and chest as I clenched around Frankie, with him gasping in my ear.

Aftershocks shuddered through me for what seemed like ages. I grunted as Frankie withdrew, then squirmed as his cum dripped out of me. It wasn't the most comfortable feeling, but good all the same.

"I'll get a cloth," he said.

"I'll come with." I cracked my eyes open to see Teague holding a jizz-covered hand above the bed as he got out. "I need to wash."

"I could lick it off for you." I couldn't see Frankie, but I heard the teasing eyebrow waggle in his voice.

"Ew. That isn't better."

"You could wipe it on the sheets. We'll have to change them anyway."

"Ew. No. Turn on the water for me, would you?"

Their banter faded as they entered the bathroom attached to Teague's room, and I let my eyes close again.

Mates are good, my bear rumbled happily.

I couldn't agree more.

THE LODGE'S great room was a *mess.*

I surveyed the upended armchair, the two smashed end tables, and the lamp that had landed on the rug and not the floor, thereby saving itself, and shook my head fondly. There was no way I could be mad, not when the damage had been caused by overzealous shifting when the curse had been broken. I couldn't say I wouldn't have done the same, overwhelmed with the urge to reconnect with my bear as soon as possible. Furniture be damned.

The claw gouges in the floor might be a little more difficult to fix.

Keelan appeared beside me, dressed in their normal version of casual—a flowy, gauzy blouse over leggings, with a loose knitted vest thrown on as a nod to today's colder-than-usual temperatures. Now that I knew the truth of their identity, I wondered how I'd never seen it before. The signs that they weren't human were subtle, but there—the way they moved was too graceful, their facial structure was slightly off, and their eyes were too...something.

So I couldn't itemize all the ways they screamed *non-human*. Sue me.

Instead of acknowledging their presence, I strode forward to right the chair. Lifting it didn't take nearly as much effort as I expected, a definite benefit to the end of the curse. My senses were sharper and I felt powerful like I hadn't for decades. It was amazing.

Keelan joined me as I started gathering the remnants of the tables. "Will you forgive me?"

I grunted. Truthfully, I hadn't decided yet.

They sighed. "I feel as though I should try to explain, but it will sound like I'm making excuses."

I grunted again. "Go get a box for this shit, and I'll hear you out."

A smile flickered over their lips, and they glided off without a protest. In moments, they were back with a sturdy cardboard box big enough to hold the bits of shattered wood.

As we started piling the wood in the box, they said, "We met by chance, you and I."

"Bullshit."

They shook their head, their long hair drifting around their shoulders. "I swear to you. Do you honestly think I would have willingly sabotaged my car on that road through the wildlife preserve on the off chance someone—you—would come by?"

I tossed a partial table leg into the box, satisfied with the clatter it made. "I don't know, Keelan. I don't know anything anymore."

They drew in a breath, held it, and let it out. "It was not a setup. I offer you my word and my full name as I swear everything I'm about to tell you is the truth. Caolán Feidlimid Cuidightheach."

Power reverberated in their name, and I didn't doubt now that what they'd said was the truth. Everyone knew there was magic in knowing someone's full name. Not that I'd be able to pronounce theirs any time soon. "That's a mouthful. I think I'll stick with Keelan."

Their smile flickered back to life. "Fair enough."

"So our friendship was real?"

"*Is* real," they corrected me. "You helped me on the road that day, then gave me a place to stay—I'm indebted to you, but more so, I like you. You're a good man."

"But not good enough to share the truth."

They sighed. "Would you have believed me?"

I considered that for a moment. Until we'd moved here and faced Muirloch, I'd assumed that the fae and their brethren were nothing more than myths. If I thought of them at all. I wasn't sure what Keelan could have shown me to convince me otherwise. "Maybe not."

"But perhaps if I'd shared my identity with you, you would have been better prepared for"—they waved a hand vaguely—"this."

I crossed my arms. "Okay, the whole story."

They gestured to the sofa, and we took seats on either end, turned so we could face each other. Their long fingers twined together for a moment, almost nervously, if I didn't know better.

Hell, maybe I didn't.

"I'm rather young by my people's standards," Keelan started.

I snorted. "What, only five hundred years?"

"Six hundred, actually."

My mouth dropped open. "What? Shit, I was joking."

They smirked. "But considering the oldest of my people can only estimate their age to the closest millennia..."

I couldn't even comprehend that.

"I'm still in my exploring and experiencing stage," Keelan continued. "We don't often try to influence humans anymore—our era has passed. But we still like this world. It has so many joys, and I wanted to experience them myself."

"Clearly, iron doesn't pose the problem the legends would have us believe it does."

"No, thank the gods. It would be awfully difficult to get around if it did." They plucked at their blouse, where it was draped over their leg. "So I crossed paths with you and was struck by your kindness despite the curse that could have turned you into a horrible, bitter person. You opened your home to me and welcomed me into your family. The very least I could do was try to help you find a cure."

"If you had been open with me about who you are..." I trailed off, unsure if I wanted the answer to the question I was about to ask but needing to know. "Would you have been free to cure me with your magic?"

"No." They shook their head. "That was never within my ability, I promise you."

A slow breath shuddered out of me, and I nodded.

"I couldn't even modify it to help with some of the effects." They sounded frustrated at that fact.

I frowned. "But the brothers' aunt modified the curse Muirloch laid on them."

"It was newly set, and she was an exceptional witch, by all accounts. She also shared blood with them, which may have made her magic in regard to her nephews even stronger."

I tilted my head in acknowledgment. "Makes sense."

"What I could do was try to help you find a way to lift your curse yourself."

"The prophecy."

Keelan chuckled and hung their head. "It was a terrible rhyme."

"Did you know what 'lead you home' truly meant?"

Their gaze met mine, and their oddly inhuman eyes were filled with regret. "I did. I'm sorry."

"So you knew all along that I was going to die." I sucked in a breath and held it. "Did you know how?"

"No." They grimaced, then amended, "Not with any certainty. I knew there was some sort of outside influence, but—"

"Holy shit. The soul bond." I stared at Keelan in sudden shock. "Did you bind Teague to me even knowing I was going to die and he would—"

Keelan reached over and gripped my bent knee. "Hush. There was no soul bond."

"There...what?"

"It was a lie. Something to make the brothers think twice about attacking you if they found out the truth. I would not, could not, do that to either you or Teague."

"But, I thought—"

"If your soul was bound to Teague, you wouldn't have recognized Frankie as your mate."

"He said he felt it."

Keelan shook his head. "Perhaps he thought he did, but I have to wonder if he felt it *before* the 'truth' came out."

I blinked, my mind whirling with all the half-truths and assumptions that had cluttered my thoughts for weeks. Months. "So that ceremony we put on for the brothers…"

"Everything about it was fabricated. A light show, if you will."

I leaned forward, cupping my forehead in my hands, as I tried to get my brain around it all. It wasn't like I thought Keelan was lying—now—but this new version of the truth was hard for me to grasp after believing something else for so long. I rubbed my temple, then looked up. "You didn't think I should know?"

"You were already burdened enough with the lie you'd told about being Christopher MacGrath. I didn't think the knowledge of additional lies would help."

No, they probably wouldn't have, but still. "I'm so confused."

Keelan squeezed my knee and released it. "I'm sorry, Chris. Truly. I know I've damaged our friendship, but I hope…we can repair it?" The earnestness in their voice was compelling enough that I wanted to assure them that, yes, of course we could get back to where we'd been before all this upheaval.

But I wasn't sure.

I crossed my arms. "Why did you disappear?"

"My king had heard of Muirloch's actions and knew I was involved, even if only peripherally. He recalled me and charged me with his authority to bring her in front of him and her own king."

"Are you in trouble?"

One elegant brow rose. "Because she's dead? No. They see it as I do. Teague's execution of her is rather poetic. Also five hundred years past due."

"So they're not going to come looking for any sort of...I don't know, revenge?"

Keelan laughed. "Gods, no. Your time of dealing with the Tuatha Dé or Fomorians is at an end. Except for me, perhaps?" Their expression was guarded, but I could see the hope in their eyes.

I grunted. "Bringing me back from the dead went a long way to making up for the lies, but there's still some work there. How are you going to do that if you're not around, eh?"

Instantly, their face brightened, and I realized that, yeah, Keelan wasn't old at all. "I *will* make it up to you."

"All I need is the truth and time." I held out my right hand.

Instead of shaking it, Keelan grasped my forearm, and I mimicked them. "You'll have both. I promise."

Chapter 24

Frankie

I was happy. I *was*. Everyone was safe, the curses were broken, and there didn't seem to be any repercussions for our activities at Garrison's mansion. It had been nearly a week since the firefight, and no one had come knocking at our door—police or otherwise. There hadn't even been any mention of it in the local news. So either the police were keeping the details close to their chests, or Keelan had influenced something. Somehow. Either way, I'd take it because it meant Chris, Teague, and I had the space to settle into our version of normal. As normal as two shifters and a magical human could get, anyway.

So why was I sulking, alone, in a tree deep in the woods?

I flicked my tail and gave a huff at my own stupidity before pressing my chin to the thick bough I was draped on. I should be over the moon. I should be rocking my mates' worlds in bed—or at least one of them. But I couldn't shake this darker feeling that had taken up residence in my brain. Hell, I couldn't even identify it. I wasn't angry. I wasn't sad.

Those two I knew one hundred percent. Maybe if I ran through all the possible emotions, I'd be able to figure it out through process of elimination.

Something shook my tree, and I snarled. Looking down, my lips immediately lowered over my teeth as I saw what had interfered with my brooding—an eight-hundred-pound grizzly. A.k.a. Chris. Next to him was Teague, looking up at me with concern. How far in my head had I been to miss their approach?

Teague shrugged off the backpack he was wearing and held it up. "I've got clothes for you. We need to talk."

We need to talk. The four most dreaded words in the English language. For a second, I thought about leaping to another tree and escaping, but Chris would simply follow. He might be big, but he could almost keep up with me, running full out. Not that he'd be able to do that in the thick woods. But, if I ran, that would give the two of them the wrong message.

Though I didn't even know what message I wanted to give them.

Gods, my brain was messed up.

Reluctantly, I rose from my perch and leaped to the ground, then shifted into my human skin. Though still wintry, the weather was warmer than it had been, with the sun trying to appear through the forest's canopy. Even so, I was thankful for the clothes Teague pulled out of the bag and handed over, and especially thankful for the runners he produced from the bottom. Chris was getting dressed too, which, honestly, was a shame. I could ogle his hairy chest all week long and twice on Sundays.

As Chris finished shrugging on his flannel shirt, he fixed his warm brown eyes on me. "Okay, spill."

Before I could say anything, Teague whipped a blanket out of the backpack and shook it out. My frown—the one I hadn't realized I was wearing—morphed into a fond smile as I realized he'd thought of everything for a mid-forest heart-to-heart.

Gods, I loved him. I loved them both.

Why wasn't I overflowing with happiness?

I helped straighten the blanket, then sank onto it, sitting cross-legged. *Spill.* As if it was that easy. I sighed. "I don't know."

Teague poked my knee with his outstretched foot. "Want me to help?"

I shrugged. "Sure. It's not like I've been able to figure out what I'm feeling on my own."

His gaze turned distant, unfocused. I couldn't feel him poking around, but that wasn't anything unusual. Teague's magic was always undetectable, which made it that much more effective.

After a few seconds, he returned to himself and gave me a small smile. "You're angry."

I gave him a look of disbelief and shook my head. "No, I'm not."

"Oh yeah. Very, very angry."

"Fuck off. I'm not." I rolled my eyes at his arched brow and turned to Chris. "I'm not."

Chris lifted both hands, palms out. "Teague wouldn't make that up."

No, he wouldn't, but I wasn't angry. I'd know if I was, wouldn't I? That was an easy emotion to identify. Besides, what did I have to be angry about? Nope. I shook my head vehemently. "Not angry. Try again."

Teague simply leaned back on his hands and remained

quiet. Like he knew everything. Like he was always right. Like...like...

I gritted my teeth. "You don't always know what's best for everyone."

"I never said I did."

"Oh no? What about at the cabin?"

His holier-than-thou expression darkened. "How would going up against eight RCMP officers have been good for *anyone?*"

"That's not the point." I gripped my knees, fighting the urge to let my claws out. "The point is you don't always get to decide that."

"Bullshit. When it comes to the safety of both of you—"

"We're adults, Teague," Chris interjected softly. "We're not your brothers."

Teague pressed his lips into a thin line for a second, his blue eyes intense. It was still odd to see them without the faint tinge of purple, but that had disappeared with his curse. "If you think I'm going to let either of you run into harm's way without thinking—"

"Who says I wasn't thinking?" I demanded.

"Were you?" Chris challenged.

"Don't think you're innocent in this," I growled. "I know who knocked me out."

The bastard didn't even look sorry for that either.

I jumped to my feet. "If you won't even admit that what you did was wrong, then what's the point of any of this?"

"What about you?" Teague shot back, getting up as well. "Do you think running off to Muirloch without a word was the right thing to do?"

"No!" Heaving a breath, I hugged myself, then said more calmly, "No."

Chris remained seated and pulled over the backpack, rooting around in it until he drew out a plastic baggie of grapes. One of the things that had changed with him was a constant surge of hunger. He was always snacking. He popped a grape into his mouth. "You're mad at yourself," he observed between chews.

I drew in another deep breath and plopped down. "Yeah."

After a second, Teague reclaimed his seat. "I think we can all agree making a deal with Muirloch wasn't the best plan."

I narrowed my eyes. "But how was that different from what you two did at the cabin? You didn't talk with me. You made the decision and acted. I was only trying to keep you both safe."

Teague and Chris exchanged a glance, then Teague scooted closer and reached for my hand. I gave it to him. "Because I knew my actions weren't going to result in my death. You didn't."

"It didn't matter."

"Fuck that." Chris grabbed my other hand, much less gently than Teague. "You matter. You matter so fuckin' much."

"But if I could save you both—"

"Not at the cost of your own life," Teague said.

"Never at that cost." Chris squeezed my hand. "The others told us what you were to the prides. A tool."

I looked down, biting my lip. Gods, I wished they hadn't learned that.

"That isn't who you are anymore." Chris tugged my hand until I looked up at him. "Do you understand?"

Teague's grip on my other hand tightened, drawing my

attention to him. "You aren't expendable. To Chris, or me, or any of us."

My gaze darted between them. There was no mistaking the sincerity in their expressions. The seriousness of their words. But at the same time...it was hard to believe I wasn't replaceable. I always had been. Intellectually, I knew things were different here, but deep in my heart, in my gut, it was hard to accept.

Chris reached out with his other hand to cup my cheek. "No more sacrifices."

"None," Teague reiterated.

After a moment, I nodded. "Okay. But you have to agree to not make decisions for me. Both of you. If I'm not an equal in this relationship, then it's not...not a relationship I want to be in." My insides quaked as I spoke my truth, but they were soothed as both Teague and Chris nodded.

Chris popped another grape into his mouth. "Was that a fight? Our first fight?"

Teague wrinkled his nose. "If we count the cabin, maybe our second."

"Cool." Chris nodded. "Does that mean we can kiss and make up now?"

"Not yet. I've got something to say." Teague inhaled deeply, as though he were bracing for battle. "I love you, Frankie."

I could have melted at the sweet earnestness of those words.

Chris smiled, but I could see the sadness in his eyes that he wasn't included in that statement. He opened his mouth to say something, but Teague cut him off.

"And I love you, Chris." He cupped Chris's cheek, his fingers scratching through our bear's beard. "I'm sorry it took so long for me to get there."

Chris leaned into Teague's touch, his eyes closing. "Not long at all, not when we've got our lives together."

Teague leaned in to kiss Chris, something more than a peck but not too deep they lost themselves in it. When they pulled back, I shot Teague a smirk.

"Oh no," he said immediately. "What—"

I launched myself at him, and the three of us proceeded to make good use of the blanket and the privacy of the woods.

IT TOOK me a few more days to recognize another reason I wasn't overflowing with happiness yet.

I didn't know who I was.

Not in the soap opera *I've lost my memory, oh noes* sense. Gods, wouldn't that be the drama-llama cherry on top of the shit sundae. No, it was the fact that I'd never truly been allowed to discover who I was, what I wanted, what I could do beyond being ordered about. I mean, I was sneaky and resourceful—I'd had to be to carry out some of the tasks I'd been given—but other than that?

Who was I?

When I confessed that the question was weighing on me, Teague and Chris insisted I had time to figure it out. It wasn't like I had to know this instant what the rest of my life would hold. They also made it clear that if all I wanted was to help run the household, that was cool. But I knew immediately that wasn't for me. What was for me was the question. And the reason I was curled up beside the fireplace in Teague's den with my laptop open to the local college's course calendar.

The only program that seemed at all interesting to me

was the social worker one. The idea of helping people who didn't have a supportive family—like how I'd grown up—was appealing, but I wasn't sure I wanted to relive the hardships I'd gone through as a kid. Or maybe it would help me put all of that to bed, once and for all. Ugh. I needed to sleep on it.

I perked up at the sound of tires on the gravel drive and spotted Teague's car trundling toward the house. He'd gone into town to meet his boss at the station to discuss...things. All the things. As usual, he'd been stoic and unexpressive when he left, so I had no idea what to expect when he returned. He hadn't shared much about the purpose of the meeting. As far as Chris and I knew, this was the *I'm sorry, we have to let you go* talk.

I wished Chris was here, but he was at the ranch, meeting a contractor with his sister to plan out building a new wing on the lodge for all the cubs they were expecting to happen in the next year or so. He was so freaking happy at that prospect—seeing all his nieces and nephews and second and third and whatever cousins—there was no way Teague or I would have asked him to be here to hear Teague's news instead.

If Teague needed support, I'd be that for him until Chris could come help.

I put my laptop aside as Teague entered the den. It wasn't nearly as large as the one in the lodge, only big enough for a decent-sized desk and the armchair I was currently occupying. If Chris were here, I probably would have let him have the chair while I shifted and lay near the hearth. Teague tossed his keys onto the top of his desk, next to his closed laptop, and leaned his butt against it, facing me. His expression gave nothing away. That...wasn't good.

If it was good news, he wouldn't be holding it back, would he?

"Well?"

"It was...interesting."

I let out a frustrated grunt. "Good or bad interesting?"

He shrugged.

Shit. "They fired you, didn't they?"

Finally, his blank expression cracked into a blinding grin. "Promoted me, actually."

"What?"

"The chief felt I had a unique take on being wrongly accused, so you're looking at Arrington PD's newest—and so far, only—internal affairs detective."

I hopped out of my seat and into his embrace, squeezing him hard. "Holy shit. Congratulations!"

"Thanks. I mean, it was a strategic move on the chief's part. A way to show confidence in me without making it look like it was a pity promotion."

Pulling back, I asked, "Pity promotion?"

"Yeah. Like if he'd promoted me to major crimes—that would've been viewed as a reward or an oops, don't sue us bribe. IA, though? Who dreams of being in internal affairs?"

"Is this what you wanted?"

He tilted his head back and forth. "Yes and no. Off patrol, yes. Without my stone skin, I'm vulnerable, and I want to make sure I can come home every night to both you and Chris." He stroked my hair. "Not crazy about internal affairs, but we'll see how it works. If nothing else, it's a higher pay grade, and at least the dirty looks I've been getting will be well-earned in this role."

I grimaced. "That's not fair. You didn't do anything wrong."

"I know. Perhaps this role won't suit me. There's

nothing that says I have to stick with it forever. There are other careers out there."

"But you love being a cop."

He tugged me closer and laid his cheek against the top of my head. "I love both of you more."

I would never get tired of those words.

Epilogue

Teague

ot quite two years later

My brothers and I watched the sunrise the day after we were supposed to turn to stone. There was nothing special about the sun appearing in the sky—the clouds lightened from indigo to violet, then lavender, fuchsia, rose, peach, the transition between each hue subtle but unmistakable. Around us, birds greeted the sun, their songs filling the crisp spring air along with the scent of the first flowers of the season. For everyone else, it was a normal Tuesday in May.

For Drew, Rian, and myself, it was a new beginning.

We hadn't planned this night-long vigil, but I hadn't been surprised when they'd settled into chairs on the patio beside me sometime around midnight. Our partners remained elsewhere, which was perfect. At least our better halves—or, in my case, my better two-thirds—would be well rested.

A part of me expected that all-too-familiar urge to overtake me, the one that made me stand where I'd be out of the way as sleep settled over me. But it never came. In my head, I'd known the curse was broken—the disappearance of our gargoyle selves, and Drew's wings, Rian's horns, and my tail was proof enough of that. Part of me, though, had dreaded this day because what if it was only partially broken? What if?

Drew leaned forward, his elbows braced on his knees and his face cupped in his hands. "It's over. It's really, truly over."

Clearly, I hadn't been the only one beset by doubt and worry. Damn, we needed to get better at talking to each other about this stuff.

On the other side of me, Rian was beaming, his eyes closed as the rising sun filtered through the trees to shine on his face. There wasn't any warmth to it yet—too early in the season and the day—but the faint light glinted in his red hair, making it look as though it was seconds from flaring alight. "Logan told me I had nothing to worry about, but..."

Drew chuckled and sat up. "Josh too."

"It was Chris who told me, over and over. Frankie refused to even acknowledge the idea."

"Because it was too dumb to contemplate." Drew smirked. No doubt he'd heard Frankie yell those exact words at me. My fiery mate was not shy in sharing his opinion.

"On this side of sunrise, it does feel like it was silly to worry about," Rian admitted, opening his eyes.

"I think we're allowed some PTSD tendencies about it."

All of our mates understood that, because they were kind, loving men. Patient too. With this hurdle out of the way, I finally felt like the future was ours to make, and the first thing I wanted to do was make my relationship with

Chris and Frankie legal. From the love pouring off my brothers, I knew their thoughts were angling in the same direction.

"I wish Odhrán was here." Rian's voice was barely above a whisper.

Drew grunted. "Not Finnian?"

"Well, of course, Finnian. But I wouldn't wish for him to have missed Elizabeth." Rian smiled, but there was a touch of sorrow in his eyes. "I'm so glad he found her. Not just for him, but for us, so we knew it was possible."

I thought back to the conversation I'd had with Logan years ago and knew there was no better time than this to share the secret I'd inadvertently kept. I directed my gaze to the ground and cleared my throat. "Finnian was alive when I woke early."

Before either Drew or Rian could say anything, I rushed on, telling them how shocked we'd both been that I had awoken two years before I'd expected to. Finnian had been in poor health, and I'd been saddened by the fact the house wasn't teeming with his grandchildren and great-grandchildren and to find out that Elizabeth had passed ten years before. But then I shared the good—Finnian's stories of his life and adventures with Elizabeth and how they'd traveled frequently around the world, especially within Canada. I told them of the love still in Finnian's voice as he spoke of his late wife and the joy that lit his faded blue eyes as he recounted all the fun they'd had. I kept talking until the sun was well up and we could hear people moving in the kitchen beyond the patio door, and my voice was nearly hoarse from speaking for so long.

When I finally stopped, Drew shook his head and wiped surreptitiously at his eyes. "And you didn't think we'd want to know all that?" I'd expected anger to radiate off him—he had the hottest temper of all of us—but instead, he seemed...content.

"It was so hard watching you both wake up and realize, *again*, that everyone was gone." I scuffed the toe of my runner across the patio stones. "I thought if I told you, I'd hurt you. Or make you feel like I was rubbing your nose in it. I don't know."

"You were being Tadgh, our big brother." Rian reached across my shoulders and tugged me sideways in a partial hug. "Protecting us, as always."

"I suppose I was."

Drew blew out a slow breath. "I think you were right to hold on to that. I don't know if I would have been able to hear it with an open and...and *happy* heart before Josh."

"Even now, it's bittersweet," Rian said with a sigh. "I wish we'd been around to experience all that with him. But I'm so glad he had a full and loving life."

"Me too." I reached out with both arms and mimicked what Rian had done a moment ago, grasping my brothers' shoulders and pulling them close to me. "It's our turn now, yeah?"

Drew shot me a wide grin. "*Ó Raghailligh Abú!*"

I shared a look with Rian, and together, we answered our brother the only way we could.

"*Ó Raghailligh Abú!*"

Thank you for reading *Stone Heart*, the conclusion to the Gargoyles of Arrington series! Please consider leaving a review.

Jenn Burke

To stay up to date on what's coming next from Jenn Burke, sign up for her newsletter at www.jennburke.com/newsletter.

Acknowledgments

If you follow me on social media (and you should!), you'll know this book just about broke me—not because it was a particularly difficult story to tell, but because my day job became extra demanding this spring and ate up a lot of my writing time. But Teague's story is done and out there, and I'm so happy with this conclusion to my gargoyle boys.

A super huge thanks to my personal assistant, Kim, who has become so essential to my work I don't know how I operated before her help. Abbie Nicole did another great job editing, even though everything was last minute with this book. More thanks goes out to my readers, especially those in my Facebook group, Jenn Burke's Epic Adventurers —your continued support is everything.

And finally—always last in my mentions but never ever the least in my eyes, my family, who never fails to bolster me whenever I need it. Love you all.

About the Author

Jenn Burke has loved out-of-this-world romance since she was a preteen reading about heroes and heroines kicking butt and falling in love. Now that she's an author, she couldn't be happier to bring adventure, romance, and sexy times to her readers.

Jenn is the author of a number of paranormal and science fiction romance titles, including the critically acclaimed Chaos Station science fiction romance series (co-authored with Kelly Jensen) and the fan-favorite series Not Dead Yet, both from Carina Press.

She's been called a pocket-sized and puntastic Canadian on social media, and she'll happily own that label. Jenn lives just outside of Ottawa, Ontario, with her husband and two kids, plus two dogs named after video game characters... because her geekiness knows no bounds.

Jenn is represented by Deidre Knight of the Knight Agency.

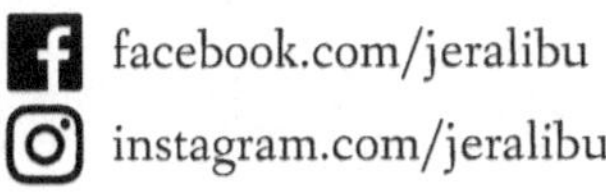

Also by Jenn Burke

The Gargoyles of Arrington

Stone Wings

Stone Skin

Stone Heart

Not Dead Yet

Not Dead Yet

Give Up the Ghost

Graveyard Shift

Ashes & Dust

All Fired Up

House on Fire

Out of the Ashes

Golden Kingdom

The Gryphon King's Consort

The Dragon CEO's Assistant

Chaos Station (with Kelly Jensen)

Chaos Station

Lonely Shore

Skip Trace

Inversion Point

Phase Shift

Jumping the Bull
Must Love Dogs...And Magic
The Sheriff of Shard Hills

www.ingramcontent.com/pod-product-compliance
Lightning Source LLC
Chambersburg PA
CBHW030929210726
48290CB00007B/2123